THE BILLIONAIRE'S HEART

WEALTH AND KINSHIP - BOOK 1

APRIL MURDOCK

CONTENTS

APRIL MURDOCK   *The Billionaire's Heart*

Chapter 1	3
Chapter 2	11
Chapter 3	17
Chapter 4	25
Chapter 5	33
Chapter 6	41
Chapter 7	49
Chapter 8	57
Chapter 9	65
Chapter 10	73
Chapter 11	81
Chapter 12	89
Chapter 13	97
Chapter 14	105
Chapter 15	113
Chapter 16	121
Chapter 17	129
Chapter 18	135
Chapter 19	143
Chapter 20	147

APRIL MURDOCK   *Preview - The Billionaire's Hope*

Chapter 1	155

APRIL MURDOCK   *Preview - The Billionaire's High School Reunion*

Chapter 1	165

Want a Free Book?	175
About April Murdock	177

This is a work of fiction. Any references to names, characters, organizations, places, events, or incidents are either products of the author's imagination or are used fictitiously.

THE BILLIONAIRE'S HEART

WEALTH AND KINSHIP - BOOK 1

APRIL MURDOCK

Adam

I could tell something was going to happen as soon as I walked into the restaurant and saw Loukas, Silas, Zachary, and Tanner already sitting at the table, drinks in hand looking smug with themselves. There wasn't one time I could think of when my cousin Loukas Mikos had arrived early or even on time for anything. He was known for being a party animal and age hadn't changed him. As I walked over to them seated at a glass round table in the middle of New York's newest restaurant, Zolo, they all lifted their drinks and cheered.

"Hey! Finally, you made it." Loukas stood up and side-hugged me as I returned the gesture. "I was about to send out a search party. It's not like you to be late." My cousin was far taller than myself and his imposing stature often meant people did things for him they wouldn't normally do.

"And it's not like you to be on time! Has the world ended? Did hell freeze over?" The guys all laughed as they heard my little jokes and I took my place at the only empty seat.

"Did you get held up at work?" Silas, my younger brother, leaned over and inquired about my tardiness.

"Yeah, he couldn't find any more gullible rich people willing to invest in his crazy 'get rich quick' schemes!" Zachary shouted across the table and the whole table erupted into laughter. I didn't mind Zach taking a low blow about my work as a venture capitalist as it was easy to make fun of him about his own dubious job.

"Exactly! All the crazy rich people are buying up all the blood diamonds they can get their hands on. How's that going, Zachary?" Again, the table cheered as we exchanged our quick jibs at each other. Zachary Lewis was my closest friend from university. We'd met each other on the very first day when we were young fresh-faced freshmen and had remained friends ever since. Over the years, his cousin Tanner Lewis had also joined our circle of friends despite the fact he was a model and stole all the ladies from us.

"Now seriously guys…what's going on? I know it's been awhile since we all caught up, but we've never met at such a civilized time or place before." In truth, I hadn't seen all the guys together for over six months and then Loukas called me out of the blue, insisting that I turn up for a meal at Zolo. No one wanted to answer and they all sheepishly looked at Loukas.

"Loukas? What's going on?" Loukas gave out a sigh and stretched his arms which made me nervous about what he was going to say.

"Do you remember the pact?" With his dark brown eyes, Loukas looked at me seriously, which was unnerving.

"Of course, I remember the pact." Ever since the first year of university, we had all taken a vacation together, every year, no matter what—that was the pact.

"Well, we think it's time to start the pact again. It's been over two years since we've all traveled together. We think this would be good for you." I knew it was me who had broken the pact, but after Megan died, I just couldn't face going away. I could feel the atmosphere of the table quickly change from lighthearted banter to a serious discussion.

"Is this an intervention or something, because I got to tell you I'm fine. I'm not an alcoholic or a drug addict... I don't really feel the need for the group attack." I couldn't help but get defensive as they all looked at me. They hadn't been through what I had. None of them had lost a wife. They hadn't had to pick themselves up after finding out the love of their life was dead.

"No Adam, that's not what this is." Silas leaned over and rested his hand on my shoulder. "This isn't an intervention or an attack. We think you've done amazingly well with everything that's happened. We just think you could do with a vacation. It's time to get back to how things were, and this is what we've always done." I could hear from Silas's tone that he was trying to tread softly with me, but I didn't need to be handled.

"Look, this just isn't a good time for me. I've got tons going on at work. I have to think about Abby and what's best for her. You guys can go without me. I'm not trying to stop you." I threw my hands up into the air, hoping that they would accept my refusal and move on, but Loukas wasn't ready to back down.

"Adam, we made a pact. We aren't going anywhere without you and besides, this year it's my thirtieth birthday and I want to celebrate it with everyone! I know you've already accomplished that milestone and picked out your chair at the retirement home, but I'm still young and wild at heart!" Loukas downed a mouthful of his frothy beer as I thought through what he was saying. Since Megan's death I hadn't exactly been myself, but that was only natural. My priorities were about keeping my daughter, Abby, safe and happy. She was only three when Megan died, and I did everything I could to ensure that life continued the best way it could. I didn't care if Loukas thought I was boring. He didn't have a child to provide for, and he couldn't possibly understand the responsibility of fatherhood.

"I want you to have a good thirtieth... truly I do, but I just can't leave right now." I sat back in my chair thinking that would be the end of the discussion but Loukas had more in store.

"Well, we all got together and voted on this and I have to say that you lost. It's a done deal. We're all booked and heading out the day after tomorrow." Loukas paused, waiting for my reaction.

"What? What are you talking about?" I could tell he wasn't lying as everyone around the table were looking at each other nervously. I half-expected somebody to shout out that it was a joke, but they all stayed silent.

"We're all booked on one of my company's cruise liners for a transatlantic trip. We dock in Mykonos two days before my birthday and we'll spend the last week catching up with family." The table went deadly silent and all we could hear was the background noise of the other diners. I myself didn't know how to react as I was still waiting for one of them to say it was all a joke.

"Is this a joke?" I looked at Silas, thinking that my brother would be honest with me.

"No. This is no joke. It's all planned and paid for." Loukas answered me, knowing that I was going to protest.

"Well, you're going to lose your money because I'm not going. I can't leave Abby...that's out of the question." I could see my little daughter's face and the heartbreak she would feel if I said I was leaving her behind for two weeks. That wasn't a possibility in my mind, not for one second.

"We know that, which is why Abby is coming with us.

Abby and the full-time nanny, they are both booked to come along." Loukas leaned forward and looked at me with a cheeky smile. "You see, we've been planning this for a long time. We've already had your assistant clear your calendar. And Natalie is fully aware that she's coming on vacation to help with Abby. She was thrilled to be the lucky sort of nanny who gets to take a Mediterranean cruise paid vacation. And last but not least, we've told your family you're coming."

I made a mental note to myself to fire my assistant and then realized what he said about family. "What do you mean you've told family?" Silas dipped his head, knowing that I wasn't going to be pleased with the answer.

"Adam, we're going to Mykonos. We can't go home and not tell family that we'll be there. I know you have your issues with your parents, but they haven't even met Abby. When I told your mom that we are coming, she was thrilled."

"You knew all this and didn't tell me?" I turned my focus back to my treacherous brother who was keeping silent.

"I think it's a good idea." Silas looked at me like a lost sheep and I knew that Loukas had broken him. "Mom and Dad haven't seen you for too long and they want to meet their granddaughter. After all these years it would be good for you to reconnect with your roots."

I let out a sigh as I thought that was the last thing I needed. I left Greece when my father tried to force me into the family business of running luxury hotels. He never forgave me for wanting to try to make my own way and I couldn't forgive him for disowning me. Even when Megan died, they hadn't visited or called. All I got was a pathetic floral bouquet and a sympathy card. I had a dead wife and a child to raise and all I got was flowers from the people who were supposed to love me unconditionally.

"I can't believe you would all do this behind my back. You

know how I feel about going home and you know that they did nothing when Megan died. They didn't call, they didn't visit, they didn't even come to her funeral, and you think I'm going to forget all that and let them see Abby?" I looked around in every direction, completely enraged by their proposal. I couldn't believe the audacity of them to mess with my life, my family, just so they could have a vacation.

"Adam, I know you're probably mad at us... I know I'd be angry, but we had to do something. We haven't seen you for months, you don't answer our calls. I can't even get you to email me back. This is extreme because we had no other way of getting through to you." Zach looked at me with hopeful eyes. I could see he honestly wanted the best for me, and I trusted him with my life.

"I've been busy with work. You know what it's like. We're all successful here. We work incredibly hard and we don't have time to be hanging out with the guys every day." I looked at them hoping they'd add some perspective to their position.

"Actually, I play squash with Tanner every Wednesday." Zach answered back knowing that they all met up regularly despite their busy work lives.

"Yeah, I talk to Loukas on WhatsApp every other week and he visits pretty regularly when there's a cruise ship in town." Silas looked back at me and I was a little surprised to hear that he was keeping up contact with Loukas. Silas had stepped into my shoes when I left Greece and started running the family business. Thankfully, it was something he wanted, and he never held any grudge against me for leaving. He lived in Greece with our parents but visited me regularly, especially in the last two years.

I looked around the table at their faces and realized I was the odd one out. I couldn't pretend anymore that I hadn't been hiding away, intentionally avoiding their communication. I couldn't even explain why I'd pushed them away; I just knew that I had.

"So, we're going to be on one of your shabby boats for a week. And that's not meant to make me suicidal?" I said. Loukas smirked as he realized I was being sarcastic, and they all laughed.

"Luxury cruise liner, thank you very much! We've won awards and everything." Loukas shouted back as they all started making jokes about the condition of Loukas's cruise ships.

"I'll go on the cruise with you, but I can't promise you that I'll be spending any time with the family in Mykonos." I took a sip from my beer, which was refreshing on my dry throat. I placed the beer down on the table and looked at Loukas. "That's the best I can do or I'm not going."

I could see Loukas think over my proposal, but I could tell he would accept it just to get me on the boat. "That's good enough for me. I just want to celebrate my birthday in style, and I can't do that without my cousin." Loukas winked at me as he lifted his glass of beer into the air.

"To the pact and finally getting the vacation we all need!!" We all lifted our glasses and cheered. I took another mouthful of my drink wondering what I'd let myself in for. It felt like the beginning of something... perhaps the beginning of the end.

CHAPTER 2

Zoe

"Did you pay for parking?" My mom shouted back to my dad as he caught up with us at the cruise terminal.

"Of course, I paid for parking, dear. Do you think I'm a hick who doesn't know how things work?"

"I'm just saying because the last time we came to the city, you forgot to pay for parking because it was one of those machines that asked for the license plate number and you couldn't remember it. I just don't want us to get another ticket." My mom was always the worrier in the family. She didn't mean to second guess my dad; she just couldn't help it as it was in her nature. Thankfully after forty years of marriage he knew well enough to just roll with it.

"Yes, thank you. I remember. I don't think Zoe needs to hear all about our parking tickets before she boards her ship." My dad winked at me as he put down one of my cases. In total I had one large case with wheels, two medium cases, and one small carry on. At the time when I was packing my belongings for the trip, it didn't seem like a lot. But now that

I was standing at the Manhattan Cruise Terminal with all of my cases and just little old me, I wondered if I'd overpacked.

"Do you think you have everything you need, honey?" My mom also looked down at the cases but thought the opposite. She was well known for overpacking and my dad frequently teased her about packing everything except the kitchen sink every time they left the house.

"They told me that they would provide all the makeup I need, but I thought it best to bring some just in case. You know, I have particular products I like and my own brushes. I just wanted to make sure I had everything." This was the first time I'd ever been hired as a makeup artist and I wanted to do a great job. At twenty-nine, I was starting a whole new career and a whole new life. This hadn't been the plan when I married Alex, my childhood sweetheart, but after a messy divorce, this is where I ended up.

"Oh, I'm sure they'll have plenty of supplies for you. The boats will be used to having shows so I'm sure they've got it all sorted out." My dad was always the voice of reason in our family. Since I was a little girl, I relied on my Dad's calm reassuring words to get me through. Whenever Mom was in a panic or fussing about something, Dad would come in and remind her about all the amazing things we had in our lives. He'd done the same for me when I divorced Alex, and not once did he judge me for my failure.

"Oh, I just wish your brother could be here to say good-bye. Two months is a really long time." Dressed in a thick orange wooly cardigan, my mom wrapped it tighter around her shoulders as she felt the breeze coming in off the sea.

"Kurt has school, Mom, it's totally understandable that he couldn't come to New York just to say goodbye." I rested my hand on her shoulder to reassure her that I was fine. "Tell him I said to study hard, okay?"

"Okay, honey." My mom smiled back at me and I could

see the tears already welling up in her eyes. You wouldn't think that I was a grown adult, almost thirty years old, but rather a freshman going off to college for the first time away from home.

We'd always been a close family, never really arguing or having too much drama going on at home. That's how we all liked it, peaceful. Kurt was a good few years younger than me, but we were still close and he'd often talk to me about his girlfriend drama. When Alex and I broke up, Kurt offered to go around and beat him up, but it was just the reaction of a younger brother who wanted to help.

When I was married to Alex, I had been an elementary school teacher. It was the only job I'd ever had and at first, I had loved it. I was a passionate teacher wanting to help every student in my class. Seeing their little faces light up when they learned something or hearing them read just made my heart smile, but it gradually became a chore.

Alex and I tried for years to have a baby and with every year that passed by with no baby news to share, I became more and more disheartened. I couldn't understand why I couldn't become a mom when I so desperately wanted a family and would have been loving and attentive with any child I was blessed enough to have. Every day I spent with precious children who belonged to someone else broke my heart a little more. I loved the kids in my class so much, but the price was high for me.

I tried for as long as I could to be happy, to fake my enthusiasm as a teacher, but when we finally got divorced I knew it was time for a new career. A new me. I went to beauty school and decided to do something where I would have little interaction with kids. I'd always enjoyed being creative and liked makeup, so I pursued a career as a makeup artist, not really concerned about whether it would work out or not.

When I graduated from beauty school, my mom found an advertisement online for a company that hired all the staff for luxury cruise liners, and they were hiring for makeup artists. I applied simply to please my mom and was completely surprised when they called me a week later to schedule an interview. Three weeks had passed since then, and here I was ready to start my new job doing the makeup for the performers in the nightly musical shows. Not exactly glamourous, but better than I thought my first job would be. And maybe I'd have some fun when I wasn't working.

As we stood on the edge of the dock looking up at the huge cruise liner, I couldn't help but feel insignificant next to the mammoth ship. I'd never seen anything like it before. In my mind I had imagined a big white boat like something you see on the commercials with happy families walking around. But in person, the cruise liner was breathtaking. It was like a whole city floating on a white cloud. It almost defied logic that something so big could float.

"I've never seen a ship that big before." I looked up at it, overwhelmed by the thought that this would be home for the next two months.

"Do you have a map? You'll probably need a map or something to be able to find your way around. They probably have charts on the walls so that people know where they're going." My mom stood behind me looking up and thinking similar thoughts to my own.

"I'm sure somebody will be on board to tell you where to go. Didn't you say that the staff arrive today, but you don't actually leave until tomorrow?" My dad stepped up beside me and handed me my documentation.

"Yeah, that's right. It's just the staff today, so it should be fine." I breathed out as I looked down at my offer of employment and all the details for my room.

"Well, would you like us to hang around, honey? We

14

could always get a room in the city for the night and come back and check on you in the morning." My mom reached out and took a strand of my long blonde hair in her fingers.

"Thanks, but I think I'll be okay." I looked over at my dad and we both thought the same thing that she was being over-protective.

"Come on now. Zoe is a grown woman; she will be perfectly fine." My dad put his hands on my mom's shoulders and pulled her away from me. "This is exciting! You're going on a new adventure. Who knows who you're going to meet over the next two months? There could be famous people, some talented performers, and certainly lots of rich people by the size of this boat!" We all laughed, and it felt good to get renewed by my dad's optimism.

"You're totally right. This is the start of something new for me. I'm not going to let fear hold me back from enjoying this." I said the words out loud more for myself than anyone else.

"Oh, you're so brave, sweetie." Suddenly my mom's hands were on my face and she pressed her lips against my fore-head. "I'm so terribly, terribly proud of you. You have an amazing time and don't forget to call me." A tear started rolling down her cheek as we kissed goodbye again.

"You heard what your mother said, have an amazing time. We'll be here waiting for you when you get back." Again, my dad leaned in and kissed me goodbye.

I picked up as many cases as I could and made my way up the wooden stairway to the staff entrance. With the wind blowing in my face, I took one last look at my parents still standing on the dock, and with a deep breath of fresh ocean air, I walked into the luxury cruise liner.

CHAPTER 3

Zoe

When I walked through the narrow doorway into the cruise liner, I immediately lost my confidence as I was confronted with a corridor filled with doorways that led to another long narrow corridor. I turned around looking in every direction and then searched through my paperwork looking for a map or directions. A flash of white caught my eye and as I looked up, I spotted a guy walking past in a clean white uniform.

"Excuse me... do you know where the staff are meant to go?" Thankfully the man paused. He was average height with a pronounced jaw and heavyset eyes. He looked me over and I could tell he was thinking something negative.

"First time working a cruise liner?" He looked at all my luggage and smirked.

"Um, yeah. I'm not too sure where I'm meant to go?"

"What department are you? Kitchen, hospitality, performer?" I could tell he was mentally trying to guess as he answered me.

"I'm the makeup artist for the evening performers." A

look of surprise crossed his face and then he waved his hand back down the corridor.

"You'll be with all the performers then. It's back down this corridor and turn left. You'll come to a big staircase which has a map of the liner. You'll want to find the main ballroom, that's where all the evening performances are held. Behind the stage is a network of dressing rooms. Ask for Mrs. Holland, she manages the entertainment."

"Thank you, I really appreciate the help." By the time I'd given him my thanks, he'd already waved goodbye and walked away down the corridor leaving me to find my way. With my arms full of cases, I found the staircase and studied the map for directions. I was three levels away from where I should be and on the opposite end of the boat. I gave out a frustrated sigh, now knowing that I'd packed too much to handle. I really should have kept it simple.

By the time I made it all the way to the main ballroom, I was sweaty and seriously tired. I walked in to find the ball-room a flurry of activity. Scantily clad dancers walked around rehearsing steps and stretching their long legs. I walked through them looking for someone who looked like they were in charge.

"Mrs. Holland? Mrs. Holland?" I dragged my bags through the crowds of people shouting out my new manager's name. "Mrs. Holland?"

"Sweetie, why you shouting for Mrs. Holland?" A tall, very thin brunette walked over to me. She was dressed in a black leotard with a white sweater tied around her waist.

"I was told Mrs. Holland is the entertainment manager?" I paused thankful to have a rest as the brunette chuckled to herself.

"I think somebody's been telling you fibs. Mrs. Holland is one of the cleaning ladies, she specializes in lavatories—if you catch my meaning. My name's Ruby. Let me help you with your cases." Ruby took hold of one of my medium-sized cases and pulled it behind her as she walked away. I instinctively followed, not knowing what else to do. "You want Mr. Fetch. He's responsible for entertainment. What are you doing here anyway?"

"Oh, I'm the makeup artist." I tried to keep up with Ruby's fast pace, but my legs just weren't as long.

"Fabulous! That means we're going to be best friends. I love a good makeover. When you're all settled in, I'll come over and you can show me your stuff." Ruby rolled my bag all the way over to a long boardroom-style table just below the stage. "Mr. Fetch, I found your makeup artist."

A rather large round-faced man looked up. "Finally! We're in the middle of rehearsals here. I thought the agency was meant to be sending someone last week?" He looked at me with sweat covering his face.

"I'm sorry, the paperwork I received said to come today. I can get started right away if you show me where to set up."

"No. No, no." Mr. Fetch waved his hand as a refusal. "We haven't got time for all that now. We are doing a dress rehearsal tonight. Come back then and we can sort it all out." Feeling deflated, I walked away annoyed that I was already a disappointment. It was only my first day as a professional makeup artist and already I had failed.

I walked myself back out with all of my cases and found the nearest map so that I could locate my room for the next two months. If I wasn't going to be working right now, then I could at least drop my cases and explore this enormous cruise liner. Thankfully my room wasn't too far away from the main ballroom; unfortunately it was far too small for all of my cases. I lined them up against the side wall and squeezed myself past them onto the single bed next to a small round window. I could stretch out my arms and feel both sides of the wall at the same time. That's all my room consisted of, a narrow bed and tiny bathroom. I couldn't believe this was a luxury cruise liner... maybe for the guests but certainly not in the staff quarters.

I splashed my face with cold water and decided that I was going to enjoy the few hours of freedom I had before I started work. I knew the ship had a cinema, shopping malls, and various other activities that I could enjoy before all the guests arrived tomorrow. With my map in hand, I took myself off exploring and wasn't disappointed by what I found. The rest of the ship was certainly luxurious, with expensive wooden paneling and staircases that had cascading chandeliers. At one point, I imagined myself to be Kate Winslet in Titanic with Leonardo DiCaprio walking towards me in his borrowed suit and slicked-back hair. I giggled to myself as I thought about dancing in a ballgown across the shiny dancefloor and the handsome stranger who would twirl me out into the starlit sky. Everything on the liner was designed to be a fairytale and it didn't fail to please.

Out on the deck were numerous activities for both families and older people wanting to relax. You could surf on a surf-simulating machine right at the front of the boat or you could rock climb three stories along the side of the wall. As I made my way back inside, I could hear the faint sound of a child laughing. I looked around thinking that my mind was playing tricks on me, but then I heard it again. It was definitely the sound of a little girl laughing and as I tried to follow it to the source, I wondered if I had been mistaken about guests arriving the following day.

Eventually, I came across a large glass wall that had 'Kids Zone' painted across the top of it. Through the glass I could see a huge indoor play area with bouncy castles, slides, and numerous toys. I stood looking into the play area and saw a little girl happily bouncing up and down in a small bouncy castle. She was dressed in a floral pink dress that floated in the air as she jumped around. Her hair was a marvelous shade of red and her long curls bounced all around her face. She seemed to be in complete bliss playing on her own.

I couldn't take my eyes off her. I wanted to be her, and I wanted to have her all at the same time. She looked so free, unburdened by life and just enjoying the thrills that play provided. How I envied her ignorance of life and how easy it is to be a child. To have every need provided for by a parent without having to wonder who will pay the bills or who's cooking dinner. It also raised up feelings that I'd been trying to bury. How I would have loved to have a little girl just like her. I'd have braided her hair and dressed her up in sweet little dresses. I lost myself entirely as I gazed through the glass and thought about the child I didn't have.

"Hello." A deep voice came from beside me and it snapped me back into reality. I turned to see the most drop-dead gorgeous man I have ever seen in my life. That line is corny, and it's been said a million times before, but it was absolutely true. I had never seen a man as god-like as the stranger standing next to me. He was a head taller than me, had broad shoulders, and a slim figure but you could see he worked out. His hair was short on the sides and a little longer on top. His dark olive skin glistened in the yellow light. Two dark brown eyes, the color of melted chocolate, looked at me with curiosity.

"Um... um.." My brain stopped working. No exaggeration, my brain literally stopped working as I looked at him wondering if he was a Grecian god come to take me to Athens. I couldn't even think of the word 'hello' to say back.

"Are you okay?" He continued to look at me with a quizzical stare while I tried to find the confidence to speak.

"Yeah. Um, yes, I'm fine. How are you? I'm just surprised to see a child here. I thought it was just staff today, but it looks like someone thought it was bring your kid to work day." For some reason, I couldn't stop the inappropriate and downright dumb words from flying out. "I should really find her parents. It's probably not a good thing that she's just in there playing by herself. I mean, where are her parents? Do they care for their child at all?" I could hear myself trying to be funny but inside I just wanted to die from embarrassment.

"Actually, that's my daughter." He looked at me and I just wanted the ground to open up and take me whole. I was praying that the ship would suddenly capsize or just unexplainably sink, then I would have been able to escape.

"Oh. Oh, great. Then she does have parents. Whew!" I playfully wiped my brow. "And what a gorgeous little girl you have. Her hair is amazing, I've never seen such beautiful red hair. I'm really sorry about what I just said… I just wasn't expecting to see any children today. You see it's my first day and I thought it was just staff on the boat, not guests. You're a guest, right?" I couldn't stop myself from talking simply because of all the nervous energy stored up in my mind.

"Yes." He smiled and I swear my legs almost caved in as I saw his pearly white teeth. His smile was nothing short of brilliant. "My cousin owns the liner, so we came out a day early to get settled in."

"Wow, he owns the cruise ship?" My mouth dropped open as I realized I was talking to the owner's cousin and not making the best first impression.

"Well, his family owns the business. So yes, he owns this liner and all the other Mikos Luxury Liners." He seemed amused as he answered me. I couldn't even fathom being that wealthy. My parents owned a small three-bedroom home and a car that repeatedly broke down, but to actually own a cruise liner, never mind a whole fleet seemed like another reality.

"Abby. Abby." In the background, I heard the voice of a woman calling to the little girl and through the glass I watched as a young attractive brunette picked up the girl from the bouncy castle and led her out of the Kids Zone.

"Daddy!" Abby escaped the lady's grip and ran over to her father. She wrapped her arms around his leg and looked up at me with a beaming smile. The brunette walked up beside them and rested one hand on the little girl's shoulder.

"She's just too quick for me to catch!" She smiled at Abby's father as my heart sank. The brunette was obviously his wife and together they made a perfect little family. Standing there just outside the Kids Zone, they could have been the models for an advertisement campaign. They had everything I wanted and everything I was so far from having.

CHAPTER 4

Zoe

"Do you want me to take Abby back to the room?" Again, the mysterious brunette looked at the man I assumed was her husband.

"Sure. I won't be too long behind you guys." He leaned down and stroked the little girl's hair. "Go with Natalie now and I'll see you later. Okay?"

I watched this intimate exchange and honestly didn't know why I was still there. I was completely intruding on this family's alone time and yet, I couldn't remove myself from their side. The little girl wandered off holding hands with the woman named Natalie while I was left alone with her father.

"You have a beautiful family." I smiled, realizing that I should say something, anything, to not look like a complete weirdo.

He looked back at them walking away and did a double take. "Oh. Oh no, that's not my wife. That is my daughter, Abby. That's her nanny, Natalie." He smiled at me as I realized he might possibly be available after all. I wanted to screech with laughter at the importance of his marital status. Why would that even matter in the least? He'd never be interested in me!

"I'm sorry. I just assumed you guys were together." I tried to contain my delight and stop myself from asking him a hundred and one questions.

"No. We aren't. I'm… not here with anyone actually." He stuttered a little and it made me wonder if he was as nervous as I was. "Well, I am here with people… just not any one person. No partner or romantic person. Nothing like that." I couldn't help but smile as he rambled on about being alone.

"That's cool. I'm not here with anyone either." The words came out of my mouth and I immediately wanted to catch them and put them back in. Why did I tell him I was alone? He didn't ask for that information and now I was just wandering around telling handsome strangers that I'm single. And the fact that I was here to work, well, wasn't it logical that I'd be here alone?

"What are you doing here? I'm assuming that you're a member of staff, yes?" It suddenly felt a bit more official with him using the word staff and I quickly tried to shake off any romantic thoughts.

"Err, yeah. I am a crew member." I paused as I heard myself say 'crew member' and wondered what deep part of my brain that came from. Is that what I was? I wasn't sure of the official title, so I decided to just keep talking. "This is actually my first day. I'm the makeup artist for the performers."

"Wow, that must be interesting. You must get to see all the backstage drama?" He leaned in a little closer like I was about to share some juicy news with him, and I got a big whiff of his aftershave. He smelled like a lumberjack and money all at the same time.

"Honestly, I don't know yet. This is my first time on a

cruise ship and my first job as a makeup artist. I only qualified a few weeks ago." I stood there feeling like a fraud not knowing where to take the conversation next.

"Well, congratulations! That's a lot of big firsts. I'm sure you'll do an excellent job." His positivity was intoxicating, and I wanted to believe in myself just like he did. "Do you get motion sickness?" Suddenly I was thrown by his question and wondered why he was asking me about sickness.

"No, not really." I looked back with a puzzled expression.

"I'm only asking because it's your first time on a liner. Some people have a hard time adjusting to the rocking. You might want to go without dinner tonight... just in case." He winked at me and all I could think was that I'd like to have all my dinners with him.

"I'm Adam, by the way." He stretched out his hand to formally shake mine. "Adam Nicolis." I took his hand and shook it feeling a little silly.

"I'm Zoe Ross. Makeup artist and crew member." He laughed at my little joke and then turned around.

"Have you got time to take a walk out on the deck?" I'd just come in from the deck, but I wasn't going to pass up an opportunity to spend time with my new friend Adam.

"Sure. I haven't got any work till later this evening. A walk would be nice." He pushed open the door and I followed him out onto the large open deck. The weather was changeable. One minute it felt warm with the sun beaming down on us and the next a gust of wind would send a cold chill down your back. The deck was completely empty, and we had the whole space to ourselves.

"Isn't it nice without all the guests." Adam looked at me and I had to control the urge to take his hand as we walked along. "I always try to come a day early if I can. I can pick out the spots I like before anyone else is here."

"Yeah, it would be nice to go on a cruise without all the

guests. To just sail the open seas with only the staff. You could have private showings of the musical productions and you wouldn't have to wait in line at the buffet." I could imagine just the two of us spending the next two months alone on the boat. I might even get rid of the staff in our private escape.

"That would be good!" Adam paused and stretched his arms out along the side of the railing. With the sun shining down and the blue sea behind him, he looked like he was posing for a Ralph Lauren campaign. I was enjoying talking to him, but I also wondered how quickly he'd get bored of talking to someone like me.

"So, are you just on vacation with your daughter?" I stepped up beside the railing but tried to keep my distance. The last thing I needed was to fall in love with an unavailable stranger who was completely and totally out of my league. I was drawn to him and he was undeniably attractive, but I couldn't let my heart get broken again.

"It's not just me. It's hard to explain but I'm on vacation with my brother, my cousin, and two other friends." He raked his fingers through his expensively textured hair, and I noticed that he looked uncomfortable explaining himself. "You see, we all made this pact, years ago, that every year we would go on vacation together. No matter what was going on in our lives, we all took two weeks out and traveled together."

"That sounds amazing! I'd love to have friends who wanted to do that." I realized how pathetic I sounded after I admitted that I didn't have that many friends.

"Yeah. It was pretty great at first, when we were younger. We did some pretty awesome trips like, Brazil, Australia. We went to Europe a few times. One time, when we were in London, my cousin Loukas took the Underground swearing he could beat us to the Tower Bridge. We took a taxi and waited almost two hours for him to find us. Apparently, he got lost." We both laughed and it felt good to give out a genuine happy laugh. It wasn't until that moment that I realized I hadn't really laughed in a long time.

"He sounds like a lot of fun." Growing up, I didn't exactly have the funds to go traveling around the world and I always envied my school friends who'd taken a gap year traveling around Europe. My biggest adventure was getting on this cruise liner to travel the Mediterranean, and I wasn't even going to see most of it since I'd be working. Just hearing these few glimpses into Adam's life made me see that we came from two very different worlds. He was well-spoken, dressed impeccably in designer clothes, and obviously extremely wealthy. I, on the hand, was just happy if I could find a cheap knock-off handbag that didn't look tacky.

"Yeah, he is. Too much fun if that's even possible. But you know how it goes, we all grew up, got professional jobs, and grew apart. We haven't been on vacation together for a couple of years now." Adam looked off into the distance as though he was thinking about something and I wasn't sure if he was happy, or sad, or simply accepting of the circumstances that had changed since his younger days.

"I know what that's like. I used to be really good friends with my next-door neighbor, Claire. We did everything together, graduated high school, roommates in college, but she got married, had a couple of kids, and lives somewhere near Lake Michigan now." I wasn't really sure if my example related to what he said, but I couldn't think of anything else to contribute. Suddenly, my sheltered and boring life seemed insignificant.

"Yeah, it's a shame how that happens to all of us." Adam started walking again and I just followed beside him. "So anyway, my cousin Loukas was determined to get us all together again this year. He turns thirty in a few days, so we're all on the cruise traveling to Mykonos where we'll meet up with family." As he talked, I was already trying to calculate how long he would be onboard for. He was getting off at the first destination stop which meant that I only had a few days to stalk him, um get to know him, while I was trapped on the ship. My dream of us spending two months together in solitude quickly evaporated with the harsh reality that I had to stay on the liner to do my job. "Have you been to Greece before?"

"Oh, um. No." I snapped back into the conversation when I noticed him looking at me for an answer. "Please don't laugh. It's very embarrassing, but this is actually my first time outside the USA." I almost closed my eyes waiting for his laugh but instead he looked at me like I was a lost puppy.

"Seriously? That's… then this is really exciting for you!" He put a positive spin on what was obviously a crazy thing for someone my age. Most people had at least been to Mexico or the somewhere in the Caribbean.

"Yeah, it is. We didn't have much growing up, so we always spent our vacations camping or at the beach. We didn't really need to leave the country for that. And for one reason or another, as an adult I just haven't had the opportunity to travel." I looked down, disappointed with myself for not being a jet-setting, high-powered businesswoman who traveled to Milan at the drop of a hat.

"That makes sense… you don't need to feel weird about that. I'm from Greece originally and my dad was always far too busy with work to take us on vacation. So, I'd swap your family vacation memories for my absentee father upbringing any day." He smiled at me and for a moment we just gazed into each other's eyes. We hardly knew anything about each other, but there was a connection between us in some deep unknown way. I could see he felt it too and my heart fluttered under his gaze.

"Well, I should be getting back to my daughter." Then suddenly he cut it off. It was like a timer had gone off in his head and our spontaneous walk had ended.

"Oh, okay." I stepped back, a little surprised by the sudden change in gear. "Well, it was nice to meet you, Adam. I hope you have a wonderful time with your daughter and your friends. And your family, of course. I hope it's good to see everyone."

He nodded and turned to go. After just a few steps he hesitated, and then turned back to look at me. "I guess you'll be pretty busy with work but if I wanted to see you again... I guess you'd be with all the performers?"

"Yeah. We have a dress rehearsal tonight, but the opening show is tomorrow night in the main ballroom. I'll be there in the dressing rooms... doing the makeup."

"Well, maybe I'll see you around." He gave a little wave and then headed back inside. I wasn't sure whether to leap for joy that he wanted to see me again or collapse into a pile because he said, *'see you around.'* He was the most irresistible, mysterious, open, and slightly confusing man I'd ever met, but I knew if I ever saw him again, my heart would be in serious trouble.

CHAPTER 5

Adam

"Can you move down? We need one more space for Tanner." Loukas whispered to me as he hovered beside his seat.

"Surely he doesn't need a whole seat for that skinny butt of his." Zachary made a sarcastic comment as he passed me in the aisle.

"Shut up, Zach! Do you want me to sit on your lap?" Tanner took his seat next to Loukas and glared back at Zach who was still smirking.

"So, can somebody tell me why we're spending the first night of our cruise watching a musical?" Zach looked at Loukas expecting him to answer.

"Don't look at me! This wasn't my idea. You can thank Adam for this." I could feel all of their eyes on me wondering why I'd choose to watch a musical when we could be at the casino or getting a few drinks at the bar.

"I thought we could do with a cultural experience. We can drink anywhere or go to the casino anytime, but we can only do opening night at the theatre once." I didn't even believe the words as I said them, and I could tell the guys weren't buying it either. We all looked at each other and then in unison burst into laughter.

"Shhh!" Somebody behind us hissed at us to be quiet.

"Hey, it hasn't even started yet. Calm down!" Loukas looked back, irritated that he was being 'shushed' on his own ship.

"Seriously though, why are we here?" Silas looked over at me, knowing that I hated musicals.

"I don't know... I just thought it might be interesting to broaden our experiences and try something different." I hoped my answer would be enough to satisfy them. I didn't want to explain about Zoe and how all of this was just a rouse to see her again. Silas lifted one eyebrow mentally questioning my answer.

"I'm all about broadening my experiences, but I'd rather do it someplace I'm not going to see men prancing around in tights." The guys snickered as Loukas joked.

"Loukas, this isn't the ballet. It's a musical." I looked at him as he shrugged his shoulders.

"Musical, shmusical... whatever, man. It's still men wearing makeup and dancing around. Something I could go my whole life without seeing."

"Well, I like that we're doing something different. I agree with Adam that we should always be open to trying new things." Tanner ignored everyone else as he read over the theatrical brochure. "And for crying out loud, Loukas. This is your boat. You should appreciate the entertainment you're offering."

Loukas simply shrugged and frowned.

"Yeah, you would. I guess having been a model, you're comfortable with wearing makeup." Zach couldn't help making a joke at his cousin's expense.

"You know, all this protesting just makes me think you

guys don't have one ounce of culture in your oh-so-mascu-line bodies. Adam and I have no issues being here, but the rest of you are complaining for no reason at all." Tanner was accustomed to people making jokes about his previous life as a male model, but he'd turned that experience into becoming the proud owner of a very successful fashion house.

While they continued to bicker amongst themselves, I looked around the theatre for Zoe. I knew she was most likely backstage doing a performer's makeup, but I couldn't help myself from hoping I'd catch a glimpse of her. All day I'd been thinking about her cute face and wavy blonde hair. She had big blue eyes and very luscious red lips, and her features were perfect for her delicately sweet face. She was the complete opposite of me, with my brown eyes, dark skin, and almost black hair.

I'd replayed our conversation over and over in my mind. She had rambled at first, but her nervousness was cute. There was nothing hidden in her conversation or manner-isms, I didn't feel like she was trying to get something from me. It was nice to talk to someone without them knowing who I was. In New York, it was exhausting avoiding women that pursued me either because of my family name or for my wealth. I couldn't just date any person, especially not when I had Abby to think about.

"Who are you looking for?" Silas was watching me.

"No one. Just wondering when it's going to start." Thank-fully as soon as I spoke, the curtains lifted and the band started to play.

"Oh boy. Here we go!" A man dressed in a tight black leotard walked out onto the stage and started singing. Loukas playfully covered his eyes as the others giggled.

"Sshhh!!" The same people behind us hissed again.

"Look, I own the ship. I'll send you a refund for the show!" Loukas always loved to drop into conversations that he owned a fleet a cruise liner, and now he was using it as an excuse to act badly.

Two hours past of nonstop singing and dancing. I'd like to say that I enjoyed it, but I couldn't even tell you what it was about. The whole thing seemed to center around the man in the black leotard, but I couldn't decide if he was meant to be a cat or a fairy. I could hear the guys grumbling the whole way through and at one point, I was sure I could hear Loukas snoring. By the time the thing ended, everyone, including Tanner, was looking at me with devil eyes.

The crowd applauded as the performers did an encore. Loukas rubbed his droopy eyes. "Is it over?"

"Yeah, the torture has ended." Zach stood up and stretched out his arms. "Well, I don't know who to thank. Adam for getting us tickets to this thing or Loukas for allowing this on his ship." They all laughed as they stood up from their chairs.

"Okay, okay. I'll apologize. That was pretty terrible. I promise I won't plan any more experiences for us during the trip." I held my hands up to surrender, knowing that I couldn't talk myself out of it.

"Um, you're not planning any experiences for us ever! Never mind just on this trip." Silas slapped me on the back with the brochure as we filed out of the aisle.

"I don't know about you lot, but I seriously need a drink after that!" Loukas looked around to see who was in agreement.

"I think I'm going to take a raincheck. I want to get back to Abby and make sure she's sleeping okay in the new room." It was shameful but I was using my daughter as an excuse to get away from the guys. I knew none of them would protest and it would allow me time to find Zoe.

Loukas responded, "Okay, but I think I can speak for us all when I say, you seriously owe us for tonight!" Again, they all laughed as we waved each other goodbye. I walked away down the opposite end of the hallway while they headed off to find the nearest bar. I turned the corner knowing that the corridor looped round, and I'd be able to re-enter the ballroom without being seen.

I quickly slipped back into the theatre entrance and made my way to the front of the room hoping to find an entrance backstage. Some dancers were coming out still wearing their full makeup.

"Hey, do you know if Zoe Ross is back there?"

"Zoe who?" One of them paused and looked at me confused.

"Zoe the makeup artist. I think she did all your makeup for tonight?" I answered, wondering if there was more than one makeup artist or possibly more than one Zoe.

"Oh, yeah. She's back there packing up. You just head down that corridor and you'll find her in the last room."

"Thanks." I snuck past them and made my way behind the stage feeling like I was doing something naughty. It always felt exciting to be somewhere you shouldn't. Like sneaking into the locker room at a soccer game or being in somebody's office when they aren't there. The corridor was filled with dressing rooms, some with open doors, and others closed. People were walking around everywhere in and out of costume. I made my way past them all, smiling and giving little nods if they raised an eyebrow at my presence.

When I made it to the very last door, I could see Zoe standing beside a large desk that had a huge wall mirror. She was packing away brushes and pencils into a black bag. I stood in the doorway for a few moments just watching her. She was dressed all in black. A thin black T-shirt and tight black jeans, but her long blonde hair fell down on her shoulders like a waterfall. She looked up and saw that I was standing behind her.

"Oh, hey." She turned and smiled at me warmly.

"I'm sorry to interrupt."

"No. Not at all, I'm just packing away." She fidgeted and put her hands in her pockets.

"I just wanted to come back and say you did a wonderful job. Everyone looked amazing." I stood up and moved further into the room. Her face lit up as she realized that I'd seen the show.

"You watched the show?"

"Yep. I heard every single word of it. I can't say I fully understood it, but it was impressive." I was hardly going to tell the poor girl that it was atrocious and the last time I watched a musical, but I had to offer some kind of compliment. She leaned in closer and raised her hand to her mouth as though she was telling me a secret.

"Just between me and you... it was bad, wasn't it? Like, really bad." She smiled as she pulled away and all I could think about was her smile.

"Honestly, it was the worst thing I've ever seen." We both burst out laughing and it was a relief that I didn't need to pretend with her. "I made my friends come and I swear, I don't think they're going to talk to me for the rest of the trip." Again, she laughed. She had the best laugh I'd ever heard. It was full of life but not overpowering.

"Oh, you didn't make them watch it, did you? I feel so bad." She leaned back against the table as she became a little more comfortable.

"You should feel bad. It was your recommendation to come! I don't think I'm going to be able to trust you ever again." We both smiled and flirted with each other which didn't feel weird.

"To be fair, I only saw the play for the first time last night. I had no idea it was that bad and I'd already invited you." She stood up and raised her arms. "I do sincerely apologize, from the bottom of my heart."

"I'm not sure I can forgive you, that's two hours of my life I'm never getting back. And what was that man in black meant to be... a cat?" She leaned back in and gently patted my shoulder.

"I know, right? I think he's a cat. I didn't ask for details, though I probably should have. The director just told me to paint his face black."

"Well, you seriously owe me." It had been a long time since I'd flirted like this and I was surprising myself at how natural it came.

"How about a drink, then? Have you got time to go get a glass of wine?" Her offer felt easy and natural, not like a date, but just two friends catching up.

"Sure. I think I need a glass of wine after that."

"Oh, stop." Again, playfully she patted me on the shoulder as we headed back out down the long corridor. We walked to the nearest bar talking about the play the whole time until I realized that I couldn't go into the bar.

"Zoe, I can't go in there." She looked at me confused as we hovered outside the door. "Oh, I want to. It's not that I don't want to, but I ditched my friends to find you. I told them I was going to check on my daughter, so I don't really want them to see me in the bar." I wasn't sure how she'd take my excuse, but I wanted to start out from an honest place.

"Oh, you're bad. That's terrible using your daughter to ditch your friends and then not even going to see her. Shame on you." She smiled as she fussed at me.

"I know, I'm a terrible parent. But if they see us together, they're going to ask lots of questions and they won't leave us alone. I'm sorry, I didn't think this through at all." Zoe looked at me and then at the bar.

"How about I go buy a bottle of wine and sneak out two

glasses? Then we can go out onto the deck and drink it under the stars?" How could I refuse an offer like that?

"I like your style. That sounds perfect." She reached for the door but turned just before she went in.

"Okay. I'll meet you out on the deck in five minutes. I'll be the one with the bottle of wine." She winked at me as I turned to leave.

"I'll be the lonely person sitting alone."

She disappeared into the bar as I headed out onto the deck to find us two seats. The whole time I sat there waiting, I just kept thinking how easy everything was with Zoe. I didn't feel like I had to impress her, and I really liked her sense of humor. I sat and looked out into the darkness hearing only the sound of the waves crash up against the ship. Could falling in love really be this easy? The thought terrified me. I wasn't sure if I could love again after Megan, I wasn't even sure if I wanted to, but as I waited, I knew I wanted to find out for sure.

CHAPTER 6

Adam

I awoke the following morning to the sound of Abby giggling as she jumped up and down on my bed.

"Oh, I'm so sorry Adam. I was trying to keep her quiet, but she ran off." Natalie quickly followed Abby into the room and tried to get her to come back out with no avail.

"That's okay, Natalie. You can leave her here. We'll be out in a minute." I waved for Natalie to go back out of my bedroom. As soon as the door closed, I quickly reached up and grabbed Abby around the waist, pulling her down onto the bed. "Come here, you little monster!" She laughed her head off and kicked her legs into the air.

"No, Daddy. Stop, Daddy!!!" She continued to laugh despite her protestations as I tickled her.

"A little monster woke me up! Come here!!" For a few minutes we wrestled each other on the bed and then collapsed into an exhausted pile beneath the covers.

"Daddy, where did you go last night?" Abby looked up at me and all I could see was Megan's beautiful eyes staring back at me. I adored my daughter more than anything, but some days it was almost too painful to see how similar she looked to her mother.

"I went to the show with Uncle Silas and the other guys." A few flashbacks of the awful musical popped into my mind as I smirked and remembered how annoyed all the guys were.

"Oh. Was it good?" Abby turned and started twiddling her fingers through my hair.

"No – it was terrible. I wish I had just stayed up here with you." I kissed her little round nose. "What did you do with Natalie?"

"We got pizza!" Abby sat up excited to tell me about her evening. "We went to a restaurant by the cinema and you could put anything you wanted on your pizza. Guess what I had on my pizza?"

"Um, broccoli?" Abby pulled a disgusted face as I guessed.

"Err, yuck! No."

"How about… hmm… tuna?" Again, she pulled a face.

"No, Daddy." She giggled as she thought about broccoli and tuna on a pizza.

"I don't know, honey. What did you have?" I knew exactly what she was going to say because she always ordered the same pizza back home.

"Pepperoni and mushrooms!" She smiled a broad smile, happy that she had out-guessed me.

"Wow! Pepperoni and mushroom pizza. What a surprise. Was it good?" I tickled her stomach as she leaned back laughing.

"Yeah! It was so good. It was better than the pizza we get at home. Can we go again tonight?"

"I'm not sure what we're doing tonight, but I think you probably need to eat some vegetables tonight." Abby frowned dramatically at the thought of eating vegetables. "Daddy, I'm hungry. Can we go get breakfast?"

I had no idea what the time was and as I looked around the room, I realized there wasn't a clock on any of the walls.

"Didn't you have breakfast with Natalie already?" I reached over to the side table for my watch.

"No, Natalie said we had to wait for you, and you've been asleep for ages!" I looked at my watch and realized it was already nine thirty, way past Abby's normal breakfast time. And much later than I normally slept.

"I'm sorry. I didn't realize you were waiting for me." I sat up and kissed Abby on the forehead. "Why don't you go and wait with Natalie. I'll get dressed super quick and then we will go get some breakfast. Okay?"

"Okay." Abby hopped off the bed, happy that she had woken me up and was finally going to eat something. While Abby went into the main room to watch TV, I jumped into the shower wanting to freshen myself up.

I was impressed with the quality of the bathroom. The floor was a black polished marble with stainless steel features and a powerful shower. I soaked myself in the hot water and immediately felt relaxed as the water pounded onto my shoulders. I was tired from the late night I'd had with Zoe, but at the same time exhilarated. This vacation was exactly what I needed, and I hadn't even known it. It felt good to be away from the familiar sights of home and to be thrown into something completely different with new people.

Zoe and I had sat out on the deck sipping wine in our stolen glasses for a couple of hours until the bottle was empty. We sat under the moonlit sky looking up at the stars and trying to name as many constellations as we could. Neither of us was sure if we were right, and we just aimlessly pointed to stars and made up our own names for them. As it got colder and colder, we huddled closer and closer together until we were snuggled right up next to each other. Even with my eyes closed, I could still make out Zoe's delicate face in the dark blue light. She was so different from Megan that it surprised me that I liked her. Zoe was carefree, breezy, and very easy to talk to. She added humor or a sarcastic jibe to everything. Zoe made me laugh, and that was new. Megan had also been easy to get along with, but she hadn't really cracked jokes or made fun of herself.

I stood for a few minutes with the water pouring down my back, conflicted about my own feelings. It had been two years since Megan's death, I knew it was time for me to move forward with my life, but I couldn't help feeling guilty. I couldn't help comparing every woman I met to the love of my life even though I knew it was unfair.

Zoe and I had enjoyed one of those special evenings that are rare for a first date. We hadn't labeled it as a date, but that's what it had naturally become. We'd talked for hours about important and pointless things, shared memories about our childhoods, and talked about our upbringings. There had been a tangible chemistry between us, and yet neither of us had dared to act on it. It was a perfect evening, unspoiled by our weaknesses or my past. She didn't look at me with pity in her eyes, she didn't see me as the lonely widower, but as Adam – someone new and exciting. That's who I wanted to be. I knew that if we continued to see each other I'd inevitably have to tell her about Megan, but for now I wanted to remain the unburdened and mysterious Adam that I so longed to be.

The three of us headed down to the main dining area where the breakfast buffet was set up. Abby immediately spotted Silas sitting with the rest of the group.

"Uncle Silas!" Abby rushed over to him and jumped up on his lap as Natalie and I took our places at the table.

"Hey rugrat! I was starting to wonder what happened to you guys?" Silas hugged Abby and then handed her a piece of his melon.

"Yeah sorry. I slept in and didn't realize the time." Hoping they wouldn't ask me any further questions, I reached for the jug of coffee in the center of the table.

"I think we all had a sleepless night after that train wreck we watched last night!" Loukas laughed loudly at his own joke.

"I don't know what you're laughing at – this is your cruise liner. You allowed that to happen on your watch!" Everyone chuckled as Tanner gave Loukas some banter back. I looked around at the long table of buffet food and could feel my stomach growling. I was hungrier than I'd realized.

"I'll go get Abby some breakfast. Do you want me to get you anything?" Natalie stood up beside me and hovered for a few seconds.

"Um, no thank you. I'm headed up there in a minute. You probably couldn't carry all I want. I'm starved." Natalie walked off to the buffet table and I could feel everyone's eyes on me.

"How did an early night make you wake up so hungry? Thought you'd have had some milk and cookies to cap off the night." Loukas looked at me suspiciously while I wondered how to answer.

"No, Daddy didn't come back until really late." Abby chomped on a strawberry while still sitting on Silas's lap.

"Oh, really? And how do you know that, Abby?" Silas looked down at her as I could feel my face flushing pink. I hadn't realized that my late-night activities had been monitored. Now, I had no choice but to come clean.

"Natalie said this morning. She said we couldn't wake Daddy up because he didn't come back till really, really late." Abby smiled as she announced her information to the table. They all smirked at me, enjoying the fact that my innocent daughter had revealed my secret.

"So then, what were you doing so late, Adam?" Silas looked at me and I could feel my throat drying.

"Yes, please enlighten us on the mischief you were getting into in the middle of the night." Loukas added his coarse comment, but Tanner kicked him hard under the table. I glanced from him to Abby and then he looked down ashamed by his disrespect. Thankfully, Abby was oblivious to Loukas's meaning and was distracted by Natalie returning to the table with a mountain of food.

The insinuation put me off more than I wanted to admit. Sure we were a bunch of men, single and sometimes insensitive, but we'd always respected boundaries. These guys knew me well and I wasn't a player. Never had been, never would be. In fact, for all our braggadocio, none of us were the love 'em and leave 'em sort. I felt the need to shut the intimate nature of the conversation down as quick as possible.

"Well, if you must know – although, I don't see why it's any of your business, but I met a nice young lady and we spent some time talking on the deck." I sternly looked at Loukas. "And that was all." I could see the shock on all their faces as I sat back ready for the onslaught of questions.

"Seriously? Good for you, man!" Tanner was the first to comment, but he could always be relied on for being supportive.

"Wow, that was quick work. How did you manage that in the twenty-four hours that we've been onboard?" Zachary was probably the most surprised, having been the main person to help me through the loss of Megan. As my closest friend, he'd spent a lot of time with Megan and me as a couple and had even dated one of her closest friends. When she passed away, he was my rock, helping me to stay focused on Abby and motivating me to survive for her. The look on his face was a mixture of surprise and concern. I wasn't sure if he was happy or annoyed at me.

"Actually, we met the day before all the guests boarded." That was all I was willing to offer while I felt insecure under their intense looks.

"So that means she's a member of staff, you sly dog!" Loukas was back in high spirits and laughed. "If she works for me, then you'll need my permission to date her." He winked at me as Abby looked up. She had missed most of the conversation while focusing on pancakes dripping with maple syrup but was now slowly starting to understand.

"Daddy, do you have a girlfriend?" The table fell deathly silent as everyone waited for my answer. I could see the confusion in Abby's eyes, and I didn't want her to think that her prime place in my life was being challenged. My poor little girl had suffered enough change, there was no need for her to worry when I didn't even know what my relationship status was myself.

"No, sweetie. You're my number one girl – always." I winked at her as her smile returned to her face. I gave the rest of the table a serious look to imply that my romantic life was not a topic of conversation and we all fell silent.

"Is that who I think it is?" Suddenly Zach looked even more shocked. "Don't look now but I think Elaina Panagos is walking over to our table." Instinctively, we all turned our heads and watched as a tall, curvy, brunette approached the table.

"It is! That's Elaina. She looks incredible." Tanner couldn't conceal his admiration for her impeccable sense of style. Her hips moved elegantly like a cat's smooth saunter and her long flowing brown hair swayed as though a wind machine permanently followed her. Dressed in a simple silky white summer dress and strappy silver high-heeled sandals, she made her way over to Adam's side of the table.

"Hello boys. Remember me?"

CHAPTER 7

Adam

The whole table sat in a stunned silence as Elaina stood before us. I gave a sharp glance over to Loukas, assuming he had been the one to invite Elaina, but he returned my look by shrugging his shoulders. He clearly had nothing to do with her miraculous appearance, but I didn't believe that my ex-girlfriend had magically shown up at our table uninvited.

"Elaina! I can't believe it's you... after all these years." I stood up along with some of the other guys.

She leaned in and whispered in my ear. "I'm so sorry about Megan." She kissed my cheek and then pulled away. "I really should have been in touch a long time ago... forgive me?"

"There's nothing to forgive." I awkwardly answered not knowing what else to say in front of the whole group. Loukas, Silas, and Zach came up and took their turns hugging Elaina.

"It's so good to see you all. Why we haven't seen each other since college. Can you believe it's been that long?" The other guys appeared happy to see her as they welcomed her and looked to be holding back on the admiration. Once she was done saying hello to the guys, she turned to the table and spotted Abby still sitting eating her breakfast.

"Oh my! Adam, this must be your daughter?" She rushed over and bent down beside Abby who just stared at the pretty lady. "Hello cutie. Aren't you a little heartbreaker?" Elaina softly pinched Abby's cheek and I was amused to see Abby's unimpressed face as Elaina stood back up.

"Yes, this is Abby." I looked down at Abby as she stared at me confused. "Abby, this is Ms. Panagos. She's an old friend from school." I thought my explanation would be sufficient for a five-year-old, but Elaina obviously thought she needed to add more.

"Old friend! Why Adam, I think we were a little more than that. I am your daddy's ex-girlfriend." Elaina smiled like she was proud of the ex-girlfriend status while Abby continued to look at her in bewilderment. Elaina spotted Natalie next to Abby and quickly made an introduction.

"Hi, Elaina Panagos. And you are?" Elaina stretched out her hand and aggressively shook Natalie's hand.

"Oh, um, I'm Natalie. Abby's nanny." Natalie remained seated and the look on her face said she wasn't entirely impressed with the woman who'd crashed breakfast.

"Oh, fabulous!" Elaina appeared relieved to hear that Natalie wasn't a threat and flicked back her long hair as she turned her attention back to me. "Everyone must have help with the little ones. I don't have any myself, but I will definitely get a nanny when that time comes." Elaina chuckled to herself as she looked around and spotted Tanner still sitting at the table. I could see she was going to introduce herself again, but I reached across to save Tanner the explanation.

"Elaina, this is Tanner Lewis. He's Zachary's cousin. A little younger than us, so you wouldn't know him from our college days."

"Tanner Lewis! It's wonderful to finally meet you in person. I've heard so much about you. I know your family, of course, but it's hard not to follow your career as well. From model to international fashion designer. Well done you." Elaina gushed praise over Tanner while he remained seated.

"Thank you. I just love your dress – perfect for a cruise." Tanner offered a compliment back, but I could tell he wasn't completely in love with Elaina after she'd commented on his modeling career.

"Oh, this old thing. Thanks, I just threw it on. I spent most of my morning ironing and unpacking. Don't you just hate when your clothes get all creased from being squeezed into the case." The other guys were still standing, and they nodded along like a group of lapdogs.

"I just can't believe you're on the same cruise as us." I tried to change the conversation so we wouldn't get sucked into Elaina's world of entitled nonsense. "How is that possible? Is this just a really weird coincidence or did you know we were going to be here?" I tried to speak in a harmless tone so she wouldn't sense my annoyance.

She playfully raised her hand to her lips as though she was a coy school girl. "Well, you mustn't tell them I told you, but your parents arranged everything." She gave out a little giggle while I tried to hide my horrified expression. "You see, they want to bring in some extra help to manage the family hotels and they reached out to me. I've been the CEO of Famtech, started a few luxury beauty lines, and now I'm looking for my next project. They asked me to come see them and discuss the opportunity. When I heard you were all coming over for your guys getaway, I just jumped at the opportunity to see you all. Don't be mad that I invited myself… I promise not to get in the way of your shenanigans." She smiled seductively at the guys who bought every single word she said except Silas.

In one clean swoop, she had offended Silas by saying that our parents were bringing in outside help to consult on the family business. He stood there with his arms folded, wondering what she could offer. I, on the other hand, didn't believe a word of Elaina's excuse, at least not the business part. Yes, my parents had probably invited her on the trip and purposely put her on the same liner, but I knew them well enough to know that they would never get outside help to manage the business.

Loukas stepped forward and put his arm around Elaina's shoulder which she pretended to like. "I think I can say for all of us that you're a welcome addition to our party. I'm turning thirty in a few days and you're more than welcome to join the festivities."

Elaina delicately removed herself from Loukas's grip while continuing to smile at him. "You're so kind. I'm sure we'll all have lots of fun catching up and celebrating your birthday." She looked from me to Silas and the tension was thick. I wasn't really sure why she was here, but I had to give her credit for showing up unexpectedly when she had no idea how things would go.

"Well I don't want to intrude any more than I have. Continue your breakfast, perhaps I'll join you all tonight for dinner." She started to walk away as some of the guys waved and said she'd be welcome at our table. I sat down as they continued to watch her walk out of the room. We were all silent for a few moments. It was as though we had just been visited by a magical creature and no one knew what to say next.

"I think I'll take Abby to the Kids Zone." Natalie looked over at me and could see that the group would need some time alone to talk about what just happened.

"Great, thanks. I'll join you when I'm finished here."

"It's okay, there's no rush." Natalie and Abby got up from

the table and waved everyone goodbye as they headed in the opposite direction from Elaina. Everyone looked around not knowing what they should say.

"So, is anyone going to confess that they had a part in this?" I still didn't entirely believe that my parents had concocted this whole plan alone. They looked around at each other feeling like they were being told off by their headmaster.

"I told your parents about our vacation plans, but they never said anything to me about Elaina. I mean, I've told a lot of people about our trip. It's not like it was a secret or anything." Loukas was immediately defensive as he was the most likely person to be involved.

"They knew my plans for the trip. I do work with them, after all." Silas looked over at me. He gave me a look that said I was being unnecessarily hard on them. After all, Silas was my brother and he would have openly shared his vacation plans with them. "They never mentioned Elaina to me and I have no idea why they'd butt in like this." He looked away, shaking his head.

"I don't understand what the big deal is? Isn't this a good thing?" Zach animated his speech with his arms as he looked directly at me.

"How is this a good thing, Zach?"

"Elaina is gorgeous. She's single, intelligent, and obviously interested in you. She wouldn't be here if she still didn't have feelings for you, no matter what she says about it being for business." Zach looked at me as though I was mad. He couldn't understand why I wasn't happy to see Elaina, but it wasn't his life that my parents were trying to control.

"That's not the point, none of that matters. This is just another example of my parents trying to control my life. I haven't seen them for years and they're still trying to match-make me with their ideal Greek woman. It's beyond ridiculous!" I could feel my anger rising up as I thought about my parents back home trying to scheme about my life.

"Maybe they intended for it to be a good surprise? After all, we do all know her from way back. She's not a total stranger, you know. Maybe they thought it would be a good surprise, reuniting you with an old friend?" I gave Loukas a sharp look as he made his suggestion.

"No. This is not them trying to do something nice. If she was an old friend that we wanted to see then we would've arranged for her to be here. None of us have seen or spoken to her in years, have we? Am I missing something here?" I couldn't understand why they were trying so hard to defend my parents. It made me wonder if they had all been in on the plan. I looked at each of them with annoyance and distrust. My feelings about this trip had suddenly changed drastically.

"Adam, we didn't have anything to do with this." Silas sat up and looked at me seriously. "To be honest, I'm not happy about her being here. She said that Dad wants to meet with her about managing the business. That's my job! You think they would have told me if they were bringing in outside help." Silas folded his arms and he was clearly upset, but not for me and how these new circumstances affected me.

"Silas, ignore everything she said. It's all nonsense. There's no way on Earth they'd bring in an outsider to run the family business. They won't even take advice from someone who doesn't have a Greek name, for Pete's sake. You have nothing to worry about. It's all just an elaborate excuse for her to be here." Silas sat back and thought about what I said. He relaxed his arms as he realized he was over-reacting.

"Loukas, how would you like it if I invited crazy Mary, your first-year girlfriend who stalked you after you broke up? Or Zach, what about Sarah Clark? How would you feel if she walked in saying that your parents had invited her?"

Zach and Loukas both looked down as they slowly started to comprehend my annoyance.

"I didn't like her. She's too polished. Her dress was perfect, her shoes, and her hair. Someone that perfect is up to no good." Tanner's comment was meant as a joke, but it fell flat given the seriousness of what had just happened.

"Whatever, Tanner. You just didn't like her because she called you a model. That's a fact, though, you know? You were a model." Loukas raised his voice while Tanner sat up, annoyed by Loukas's input.

"It's just the way everyone makes out like it's something I should be ashamed of. Oh, you were a model but now you're a successful business owner – what's wrong with being a model?" Tanner did a silly impression of Elaina and finally we couldn't all help but laugh. It helped to distill some of the tension between us all.

"I know you don't want to hear it Adam, but I'm going to say it again. What's so wrong with Elaina being here? You liked her at one stage and now she's a successful business-woman who's drop dead gorgeous and apparently chasing after you. Maybe you should be thankful and not complain?" Zach looked at me and I could see he was only trying to understand, not cause an argument. The rest of the guys also had their eyes on me, and they looked like they agreed with Zach's summation.

I gave out a sigh and unfolded my arms. "Look, I'm not interested in Elaina. She's exactly what my parents want in a daughter-in-law, and I'm not going to let myself be manipulated by them or her. If you're so impressed with her, then help yourself. I just want to enjoy this trip with my daughter and you guys, without being forced into an arranged marriage." I stood up from the table, tired of having to explain myself.

"I'm going to see Abby. I'll see you all later."

CHAPTER 8

Adam

As I walked away from them, I could feel all their eyes on my back. I was sure they would be having an in-depth conversation about my failures and how I was overreacting to Elaina's sudden arrival as soon as I was out of earshot. It reminded me of why I had distanced myself from the group after Megan's death. It's hard to explain to people who haven't gone through the same thing, but I suddenly became aware that everyone was talking about me. I had become a widower overnight. One dramatic turn of events had changed my life forever and therefore changed how everyone viewed me. Instead of Adam Nicolis, the independent venture capitalist who'd struck out from his controlling Greek family, I was now Adam Nicolis, sad widower and single parent who needed help fixing his sad little life.

People saw me as a project. My sadness was unbearable for other people as it took them out of their own happiness for a moment. It wasn't anyone's fault, that's just how it was. Strangers would meet me and want to embed themselves in my life, thinking they could solve all my issues by babysitting

Abby. Even friends didn't know how to behave around me. They would talk about their love lives and then apologize, as though I was angry at them for having something I'd lost. I couldn't have a simple conversation without somebody imposing their 'widower' view of me.

As a result, I distanced myself from everyone. Zachary had been my only true friend that held me together the night Megan died. He'd seen me at my worst, broken, bitter, and angry at the world. He'd helped me organize her funeral and take care of Abby in the weeks after her death. Zach had refused to let me fail, and he fought steadfastly against my efforts to push him away. That's why it hurt even more to see his support of Elaina. I'd seen him look at me suspiciously when I was telling them about Zoe, but then as soon as Elaina turned up, he did a turnabout and vouched for her. I just couldn't understand him.

After walking off my frustrations around the deck, I headed down to the Kids Zone to check on Abby. There were a few tables beside the glass wall of the play area, and I sat myself down where I had a good view of Abby playing inside. She was sitting at a long white table with Natalie beside her. They were drawing around their hands with crayons and then coloring them in. She looked perfectly happy sitting next to Natalie and it was a little heartbreaking to see. I couldn't help but think, '*That should be your mother sitting next to you.*'

Megan had been an amazing mother. She'd had the patience of a saint, much more than me. When Abby was two, she had been into everything and we were constantly finding toys in the trash bin or food in the oddest places. It frustrated me, whereas Megan would take the time to explain everything to Abby. They would sit for hours reading books and playing with stickers. It just wasn't fair that my sweet little girl had to go through life without her mother.

Without her amazing mother who loved her beyond measure. I couldn't understand a world where Megan could be taken from us, but other people who treated their kids like afterthoughts could stay. It was all so wrong.

I wiped the tears from my eyes and slowly breathed in and out. It had become my mantra over the past two years. Any time I felt myself slipping backwards, I'd breathe in and out slowly and tell myself, *'Just breathe.'* It was simple but worked surprisingly well. Zach told me that Army SEALs did it when they were in high-pressure situations. I might not understand God's plan, but my focus had to be surviving for Abby. I couldn't let myself become a bitter and twisted person, no matter how easy it would be to slip into that place. It was harder to stay positive and constantly exhausting, but necessary if I wanted to be the best version of myself for my daughter.

I continued to watch them play for a while and as I calmed down, I thought about my parents. I hadn't seen them for so many years, yet they were trapped inside my mind still looking and acting as they had been over ten years ago. They hadn't seen the person I had become, and they hadn't even met their granddaughter. That thought troubled me and it was something that constantly haunted me.

When Abby was born, Megan and I discussed the need for me to mend my relationship with my parents. It wasn't fair that I was denying Abby a relationship with her grandparents simply because I couldn't get over the past. It had been hard listening to Megan be so blunt, but deep down I knew she was right. I'd put it off and put it off for so long that it just never happened. Then Megan died. They sent me a card and some flowers. I was enraged. It just gave me more reason to stay angry at them and push them further away.

Silas would try to talk to me about them, but I refused to listen. My younger brother lived in Greece with them, but frequently visited me. It may have seemed odd to other people that we had a good relationship while ignoring the fact we came from the same parents and had opposite relationships with them. Silas eventually knew not to mention them to me, and we simply didn't talk about them.

When Loukas arranged the surprise vacation, I had initially been mad. I didn't want to see them; I hadn't prepared myself for that. But knowing it was inevitable, thoughts had slowly crept in that perhaps this was the time to heal old wounds. Every member of my family was going to be at Loukas's milestone birthday celebration, and I didn't want to be the only disgruntled person there. Yet, after this morning's drama with Elaina, I wasn't sure if I could ever forgive them. It was all too familiar of how they had acted in the past trying to control every aspect of my life. My dad would force business meetings on me when I was completely unable to run a hotel, never mind several. My mother would push her friends' daughters in front of me and name off their achievements as though they were a product for order. It was a life I couldn't bear and didn't want.

Just as I was drifting down another avenue in my mind, Natalie spotted me and waved from the other side of the glass. I awkwardly waved back and watched as she told Abby to go and play on the bouncy castles.

"Hey, do you want to come in and play with Abby?" Natalie popped her head through the door.

"I will, I just need a little bit of time to calm down from this morning." I smiled back as Natalie headed over to my table.

"Do you mean Elaina? Yeah, I guess that was a blast from the past?" Natalie pulled out a chair and sat down.

Natalie reminded me of every 'girl next door' in the romcoms Megan had adored. She was cute and perky and most people would consider her to be attractive. But Natalie was completely focused on her job of looking after Abby. Even though she was in her early twenties, she seemed to despise technology and refused all forms of social media. This was unusual for someone so young, but exactly the type of mindset I loved for my daughter's nanny. It was a relief that she wasn't distracted by her phone or taking selfies when she was looking after my daughter.

Natalie had been Abby's only nanny since Megan had passed and the pair had become inseparable. Natalie had been studying child psychology in college and eventually planned to become a therapist, but when I explained our situation, she promised to stay with us until Abby went to school. It was a huge relief knowing that we had someone permanent in our life who could be a friend and a mother figure to Abby. Natalie had become more like a friend or younger sister, rather than a paid employee and she was often at our house even on her days off. She had a boyfriend named Jack who'd appear and then disappear for months at a time. I tried not to pry too much into her love life but hoped that she'd ditch Jack once and for all so she could find someone who treated her right.

"Yes. Elaina was a complete surprise. I'm sorry if she offended you." I recalled Elaina's odd comments about needing a nanny and hoped Natalie didn't feel put down by them.

"Oh, no. She's exactly the type of person I wouldn't work for. She'd treat her kid like a poodle, not a person." Natalie always spoke her mind which I appreciated. She turned her face in horror and gasped. "I'm sorry... she was your ex-girl-friend. I didn't mean to be so judgmental."

I chuckled as her opinion was spot on. "No need to apolo-gize. You're totally right. She would have Abby dressed up like a little doll and wouldn't allow her to get dirty. Ever. Poor kid would never have any fun."

Natalie relaxed back into her chair as she saw that I didn't take offense to her comment. "Oh man, demanding parents like that put so much stress on their children. It causes so much anxiety and issues later in life." The therapist in Natalie was starting to come out.

"Yeah, I can relate to that. My parents were pretty demanding – still are." I folded my arms and sat back, still thinking about how I could avoid Elaina during the trip.

"Did she say that it was your parents that invited her on the trip?"

"Yep. Some nonsense about them doing business, but it's just a ploy to matchmake us together. We dated for a while in college, but it didn't work out. My parents only love her because she's Greek. They completely ignore the fact that she's a narcissist." I was still in shock that my parents would do this. Even as I spoke, I could hear my anger.

"So, you guys didn't end well?" Natalie looked interested and couldn't help but wonder what I'd ever see in someone like Elaina.

"It's not that it ended badly... it just ended. Elaina was everything my parents wanted and when I met her, we just made sense. We became a couple because it was the obvious thing to do. It worked at first, while we were both young and optimistic. I was destined to take over my family's hotel business and she was destined to conquer the world of business, but I went against the plan. She dumped me the minute I turned my father down. I no longer had money and therefore, I no longer had value."

I laughed to myself remembering the day Elaina broke up with me. She didn't even say the words or confirm we were over; she just didn't say anything when I told her about going out on my own. I had all these crazy ideas about moving to New York and starting my own business without my family's help and the whole time she looked at me like I was out of my mind. At one point, she asked me to recon-sider rejecting my place in my father's business, but when she could see I was serious about going on my own, she just backed away.

Elaina had promised to call me so that we could make plans about moving to New York, but I never heard from her again. I called her a few times but didn't get any answer. It didn't take me long to realize I'd been dumped, especially when I heard through mutual friends that she was dating another wealthy bachelor. I moved to New York, met Megan, and the rest is history. And the truth is, I never missed her. I was happy to go on with my life without her.

"Wow. I guess this vacation won't be that much fun after all?" Natalie looked at me with sympathy as I leaned forward and rested my elbows on the table.

"I've been trying to think about how we can avoid Elaina. She's on the same ship, so we can't go anywhere, but if we had something that would deter her then she might leave us alone?"

"Well, you're the prize. So, all we have to do is remove you from the game. If you're not available, then there's nothing for her to win." We both thought through the logic as Natalie spoke.

"Exactly." I looked up into the air thinking about how I could remove myself from the equation.

"I've got it! You need a girlfriend!" Natalie slapped her hands together pleased with her own scheme. "Tonight, at dinner, you introduce her to your girlfriend. Have everyone play along and then she'll know you're not available."

"That's brilliant. She might back away entirely if she thinks I'm committed to someone else. But who's going to be my girlfriend at such short notice?" I looked at Natalie as we both thought the same thing.

"Not me! She already knows I'm the nanny and this..."

Natalie pointed back and forth at me. "This isn't believable. We couldn't pull that off."

"It might confuse Abby if she was paying attention, anyway. That would be very bad."

And she was completely right about us as a believable couple. Even though she knew so much about me, we didn't look like a couple at all and it would be just plain weird to act that way with Natalie. I wasn't going to risk losing my nanny just to avoid Elaina. Then, as I watched Abby jumping up and down, the answer came to me.

"I know who might do it." I jumped up out of my chair, eager to set the plan in motion. "Can you stay with Abby? I've got to go get a girlfriend!"

CHAPTER 9

Adam

I rushed off, not really knowing where I was going. I headed back to my suite and texted Zoe that I wanted to meet up. She quickly got back to me and we arranged to meet beside the deck pool. I quickly changed, freshened up, and headed down to the pool with two bottles of cold water in hand. As I headed out onto the deck, I spotted Zoe standing over by the railings in a yellow sundress. She turned just as a ray of sun broke through the clouds and illuminated her golden hair. Dressed in yellow and with her hair glowing, she just looked like the very vision of summer.

"Hey, I grabbed us some drinks on my way." I handed a bottle over to her while still admiring how perfect she looked in the sunshine.

"Oh, thanks. That's nice of you." She took a sip and then raised one eyebrow as she noticed that I was still staring at her.

"Um, sorry. You just look so radiant in this light and with your dress. It, um, matches the sun." Her cheeks immediately flushed pink as I complimented her, and it was cute to see how bashful she was. "I'm so glad you were able to meet me on such short notice." I moved in and rested my arms against the railing.

"It's not a problem. I'm only working at night, so I'm generally free during the day. Is something wrong? It sounded urgent in your message." Zoe looked up at me with her sparkly blue eyes and I felt nervous about what I was about to say. My whole plan was insane, and now that I was about to ask her to be part of it, I suddenly felt foolish.

"Well, there is something. But I should probably give you some background first." I sounded unsure as the words came out. I couldn't just blurt out my question without explaining myself.

"Okay. I'm all ears." She raised an eyebrow and tilted her head. Anticipation along with uncertainty radiated in her smile.

"This is going to sound bizarre but believe me when I say that I didn't plan any of this." Her face wrinkled in confusion and I could see she was already lost. "I was having breakfast with my friends this morning when my ex-girlfriend turned up, completely out of the blue. Her name is Elaina and we dated in college, years ago. I have absolutely no interest in her... I don't even really like her. It seems that my parents invited her on the trip. They think that because she's Greek and successful, we should be together. That's not what I want at all. So, she's here on the ship and will be coming to Mykonos with us for my cousin's thirtieth birthday party." I paused so I could breathe. I rushed through my story and wondered if I sounded like a lunatic.

"Oh, I see." Zoe remained quiet just looking off out into the sea.

"I really have no interest in Elaina, Zoe. I haven't seen her for years and would have been content to never have seen her again, but this is the type of thing my parents do. They're very controlling and won't just accept that I have made a life for myself that doesn't include their hotel empire or their social network. She just comes from the right type of Greek family, that's the only reason they're trying to force us together."

"No, I get that. I just... I just don't understand why she'd come all this way? I mean, she must be interested in you to go to all the effort?" She looked at me with a shrug and I could feel her insecurity.

"I honestly have no idea what she wants or why she thinks she's here. Even if she is interested in me, I don't care. I only have feelings for one person and that's you." I took her hand in mine and tried to look at her seriously. "We had an amazing time last night. I haven't connected with anyone like that in a really, really long time. Please don't think that this is something I do all the time, because it's not. There's something between us. Something real and I want to see where it can go."

"You really mean that?" She bit her bottom lip as she looked up at me and I just wanted to kiss her.

"I really do. This whole Elaina thing is just a complication and nothing more than that." I squeezed her hand, hoping that she would sense my sincerity.

"Okay. I like you Adam, but I'm not a leap in kind of girl. I don't do impulsive things like this. I can't get hurt again, not after Alex." Zoe had briefly mentioned her ex-husband last night and I had no intention of treating her the same way he had.

"I'm not going to do anything to hurt you, Zoe. I promise." It all felt very serious and very fast. The truth was, I truly was sure there was something between us and I did want to explore it further. Our quick connection and flirtation had quickly escalated into something very real. As we looked at each other intensely, I knew I still had my insane question to ask but I was scared of her answer.

"I do have something a little crazy to ask you." I held my breath and could feel my heart pounding furiously. "I kinda have this crazy idea to get Elaina out of the way. It's going to sound insane, but just bear with me. It might get her to back off and not ruin everything."

"What is it?" She looked up at me with a concerned expression.

"Well, if she thinks that I'm already in a relationship, then she might go away. I just need someone to pretend to be my girlfriend and that's what I'm hoping you might help me with?" As I asked her, I knew there was no way she would agree. It was completely bonkers to think anyone would agree to do this.

"You want me to pretend to be your girlfriend?" She looked at me with a slight hint of disgust. She was probably wondering why I just didn't ask her to be my girlfriend, rather than pretend. And as she looked at me, I realized that I had offended her.

"We've only known each other a day and although we have this great spark, I didn't think either of us would want to rush into a relationship immediately. I'm not saying we won't get there, I just don't think that's what either of us wants right now. And even if I introduced you as my girl-friend after only one day, the plan wouldn't work. Elaina needs to believe that we're in a long-term committed rela-tionship that won't fall apart by her sudden arrival. If she knows we've only just met, then she'll just try to split us up." I rambled like the mad hatter with my scheme.

She looked at me as if I'd lost my mind on top of being a jerk. I felt the need to diffuse the crazy.

I raised my hand in a desperate gesture. "Please, just wait.

I know this is crazy and weird, and probably a little frightening."

"Yeah, you think?" Zoe frowned and took in a deep breath. "I don't understand how you think any of this is going to work. I'm going to be working every evening, so she'll have plenty of time to hang around you. And you're all getting off in a couple of days. I'm not. How will you explain that I've decided to stay on the ship and be a makeup artist while you all go off for your cousin's birthday? Won't that look a little odd?"

I wasn't surprised by her questions; I'd been going over exactly the same scenario in my mind while preparing myself for this talk.

"That's where the plan gets a little adventurous." I looked down at the deck floor wondering if she was going to totally flip out at my next suggestion. "You wouldn't be working on the cruise liner anymore and you'd come with us to Mykonos." I left the idea hanging in the air between us.

"You're asking me to just quit my job? My first job in my new profession that I've only had for a few days. So that I can pretend to be your girlfriend to help you brush off your old girlfriend? Oh, and because your parents planned all of this." She flippantly threw the scenario back in my face so I could hear how insane it sounded.

"Zoe, I am asking a lot. I know."

"No, this isn't a lot. A lot would be asking me to take the night off or maybe taking your daughter while her nanny takes a break. You're asking for everything – my job, my time, and for what? So you can lie to your family and everyone you know." When she put it like that, I felt ashamed of myself.

"You're not wrong. I don't disagree with anything you've said, but I don't come from a loving family like you do. I don't

APRIL MURDOCK

have understanding parents that let me make my own decisions. I had to run away and abandon everything just so I could make my own life. I know I sound like a poor rich kid complaining about how hard life was at the mansion, but money isn't everything – that's why I left it all to make my own." I looked out at the sea and found a little moment of rest in all the drama.

"I know you don't know me, and you don't know my family, but I know them. Elaina being here is all part of some elaborate plan for them to draw me back into their world. I can't just be myself; it won't work. This plan is a way to avoid all of their schemes, but it also allows us some time together. We can enjoy being together for the next few days on the ship and then I'll take you to Mykonos. It's a beautiful place. I can show you where I grew up, you'll meet the rest of my family, and we can see if this has a chance to last beyond a two-week holiday romance." I could see that she was thinking it through. She wasn't entirely convinced but at least she was considering it.

"I need to think about this. I can't just quit my job. I need a job since I don't have a trust fund." Zoe started pacing the deck as I followed beside her.

"I know that. I'll buy out your contract with my cousin. He owns the ship, so I don't think any of that will be a problem. I'll give you the cash for the whole two-month contract up front and I'll pay you a fee for the next two weeks. All expenses will be paid for, new clothes, spending money – anything you need." It suddenly felt like we were negotiating, and I wasn't sure if that was a good thing.

"Now I just feel like you're trying to buy me." Zoe threw her hands in the air and stared me down. "I really don't know about this, Adam. I don't even know you and I'm considering going to Mykonos with you? I'll be a complete stranger surrounded by your family and what if things don't work out between us? What if we realize we actually hate each other?

Will we still be pretending then or are you going to send me home as soon as your plan works?"

"Zoe. Zoe!" I walked up and put my hands on either of her shoulders. She was starting to work herself up with ridiculous situations that weren't ever going to happen. "Zoe. You do know me." I looked straight into her eyes and held her gaze. "You know that I have a little girl called Abby. She means everything to me. I have a nanny called Natalie and she will be there the whole time. I'm on the cruise with my younger brother, cousin, and two friends – you'll meet them. Everything that happened between us last night was real. I really like you and think this could be the start of something amazing for us both. It's a crazy start, but I think we could have an exciting adventure together over the next two weeks." She listened to every word as she breathed in and out. "So, what do you say? Do you want to go on an adventure with me?"

"Do you promise you aren't a psychopath who's going to kill me?" She looked back at me and I couldn't tell if she was joking or not.

"I promise. The worst thing that could happen is we realize we aren't meant for each other and then we go our separate ways. That's it." She looked from me back down to the ground a few times as I remained holding her shoulders.

"Okay. I'll be your pretend girlfriend if you speak with my boss." She gave a crooked smile as I pulled her into my arms.

"Thank you! Thank you so much! I think we're going to have a lot of fun!!"

CHAPTER 10

Adam

"So, Zoe isn't your girlfriend?" Abby looked at me with her big wide eyes as I struggled to explain Zoe's new role to her. I knew this was going to be difficult, but as I tried to tell her about Zoe, I wondered if I was being completely irresponsible exposing my daughter to the sordid details of my hairbrained scheme.

"You saw Zoe down at the Kids Zone, the very first day we arrived. Do you remember?"

"Uh huh." She fidgeted as she sat on my lap.

"Well, I like Zoe and I want to spend more time with her. I'm going to be referring to her as 'my girlfriend,' but I want to know if that's okay with you first?"

"Why?" Again, she looked up at me as I fumbled my way through.

"Because you're my number one girl and always will be. I want us both to hang out with Zoe, like we do with Natalie."

"Well, then just make Natalie your girlfriend." Abby smiled and her simple answer seemed like the remedy to everything. How I wished it was that simple.

"Natalie is your nanny. She's our friend too, but I want a friend that is just mine. A friend that I can call my girl-friend... if I want to." I wasn't sure if Abby understood any of what I was saying, but I had to tell her something in case she blew our cover story with Elaina.

"Okay... so, Zoe is your girlfriend?" We had come full circle and I decided there was no point in continuing the conversation any further. The easiest thing for everyone was just to call Zoe my girlfriend and hope that Elaina wouldn't probe Abby for any more details.

"Yes. Zoe is my girlfriend. Is that okay?" Abby paused for a few seconds and I watched as her little mind thought about it.

"It's okay with me. I think it will be nice to have another girl to play with. I hope she likes coloring." Abby kicked her legs and jumped off my lap.

"I'm sure she does." I winked at her and then pointed over to her bed. "Now it's time for bed. I'm going out for dinner with the guys, but Natalie will be watching TV just on the other side of the door." Abby slid under the covers and twisted herself into a little ball.

"Okay, Daddy." She sucked on her thumb, a bad habit she hadn't been able to break.

"Night, night, my angel." I bent down, kissed her soft hair, and headed back out into the lounge.

I'd asked everyone to come over before we went out for dinner so I could go over the plan and introduce them to Zoe. As I looked at them all seated in the living area, I suddenly felt like I was George Clooney in *Ocean's Eleven* going over the plans to heist a casino. It all felt a bit ridiculous.

"Thanks for coming over, everyone." I walked in front of the TV and switched it off to get their attention.

"What's with the secret meeting? Are we taking over the

ship or something?" Zach joked as Loukas looked up a little concerned by the suggestion.

"I know my instructions were a bit cloak and dagger, I just wanted to make sure that everyone turned up." They all stared at me and I started to feel my palms sweat from nerves. I wasn't sure how they were going to respond to my plan, but I still felt like it was necessary to put it into action and clue them in.

"I've spoken to Loukas briefly about what I'm going to share with you because he had to help me with one of the details, but I've been thinking a lot about Elaina being here. I really don't want her to ruin our trip. You might not see her as a big deal or as a bad thing, but I do. I don't want to be spending my evenings with her. I don't want to be spending any of my vacation time with her. I don't want my daughter exposed to her. And that's why I've come up with a plan to get her to leave us, or at least me, alone. For this to work, I need all of you onboard. It's just not going to work if one of you breaks from the plan."

"You aren't planning on killing her, are you? Because I didn't sign up for that." Silas winked as he made his joke and the others chuckled.

"No, nothing that extreme. I'm talking more about a few white lies or one big lie. I want us all to pretend that Zoe Ross is my long-term girlfriend." I stopped talking and watched as the idea sunk into their brains.

"Zoe who?" Tanner looked puzzled and clearly had no idea who I was talking about.

"The makeup artist I was telling you about at breakfast before Elaina came over. I've asked Zoe to join us on our trip and she's agreed to come and pretend to be my girlfriend."

Silas sat up but he wasn't cracking jokes anymore. "What? You've asked a strange woman to pretend to be your girl-friend so that you can avoid Elaina?"

"I know it sounds extreme. But I was talking it over with Natalie and I realized that I need to be unavailable. If Elaina thinks I have a serious girlfriend, then she'll probably leave me alone and we can just enjoy our trip." I could see from their faces that they weren't entirely convinced.

"I think this is a bit of an overreaction, Adam. I mean, Elaina said she had come to meet with your parents about business. She never said she was after you." Zachary looked at me like I'd lost my mind.

"Oh, come on Zach. That business stuff is all lies. My parents have sent her here in the hope that we'll reunite, fall madly in love, and move back to Greece. It's just a huge scheme my parents have cooked up and I don't want to get dragged into it. If I have a girlfriend then she can't follow me around and my parents won't have a reason to keep pushing her in my face." I could see them thinking it through, but I still had a way to go to convince them. "I've spent the whole day going over things with Zoe and sorting it out with Loukas so that she can stop working. I actually really like Zoe and would be introducing her to you whether Elaina was here or not. She might actually become my girlfriend eventually, so it's not the biggest lie I could dream up."

They all sat back, a little surprised to hear me confess my feelings for Zoe. I could see them all thinking the same thing, that this must be serious if I was willing to go through with such a crazy plan.

"I don't really understand it, but if this is what you want to do, I can play along." Zach looked at me with a solemn stare. I knew he was far too sensible to ever do anything this mad, but he would be willing to do it for me.

"I think it sounds like fun. I'd rather not spend any time with that horrendous Elaina either." Tanner was in. Now it was just down to Loukas and Silas.

"You know I've already agreed. The entertainment

manager wasn't too thrilled about losing his makeup artist, but money always seems to help calm people down. You owe me big time, Adam. I'm still thinking about how you can repay me for this." Loukas winked at me and I knew he wasn't joking. He'd pulled out all the stops arranging for Zoe to end her contract and find a replacement, but he also enjoyed the thrill of the plan. It hadn't been cheap to get this going. I had to pay Zoe her salary for the rest of her contract, plus a salary for being my girlfriend, and then I'd also have to cover the ongoing expenses. Having a fake girlfriend was expensive, but I was willing to bet that the plan would work.

"I just don't know if this is the best way to go about it?" Silas was the only one not in agreement. "I don't mind keeping the truth from Elaina, but you're asking me to lie to our parents. We're going to have to pretend that she's your girlfriend in front of our whole family." Silas looked down as he thought about what to do.

"I know. I've never asked you to do anything like this before and I'm sure if we had more time, we'd be able to think a better way out of this, but it's too late. Zoe will be here any minute – I need to know if you're in?" I looked at Silas and could see the struggle on his face. He didn't dislike our parents as much as I did, but at the same time he didn't want to betray their trust. As much as I needed his help, I understood his ambivalence.

"I'm willing to say that she's your girlfriend because that may not be too much of a stretch for now since you do like her, but I'm not going to flat out lie for you. I won't go all in if someone asks me for details." Silas looked serious and I knew I shouldn't push him any further.

"That's okay, that's enough. All you guys need to say is that we've been dating for a few months, it seems pretty serious and that's it. Just keep it simple." They all looked at me in agreement as a loud knock came from the door. "That will be Zoe."

I walked over and answered the door while the whole room sat silent. "Hey." I smiled as Zoe walked in, looking stunning in a floor length red dress. I'd given her one of my credit cards earlier in the day and told her to buy some outfits for evening meals, but I hadn't expected her to look so gorgeous.

"Am I overdressed? I wasn't sure how fancy to go?" She looked up with her beautiful blonde curls falling down her back.

"No, it's perfect. You look amazing." A proud smile went across her face.

"Everyone, this is Zoe Ross, my girlfriend." I introduced her with all the confidence I had inside me. They all smiled at her and I could see they were also stunned by her beauty. "Well, let's get this show on the road!"

We headed down to the formal dining restaurant and took our seats at a large round table. Everyone seemed a little uneasy with the new arrangement and it took awhile for us to fall into easy conversation.

"So, Zoe. Tell me why anyone as lovely as yourself would be willing to play along with my brother's silly scheme?" Silas poured red wine into Zoe's glass as he waited for her answer. The whole table went silent and looked at me to react.

"You don't have to answer that." I gave Silas a stern look which implied he should back off.

"It's okay, I don't mind answering." Zoe smiled at me and I was surprised that she was willing to fight back. "I've been thinking the same thing all day. Silas, I'm guessing you had a privileged upbringing. Am I right?"

"Our family is wealthy, yes." I could see Silas was thrown by her question reversal.

"And all of you here probably come from wealthy parents

and had the best of everything growing up?" Zoe looked at them all as they stared at each other. They didn't answer but they all nodded their heads and signaled that she was right.

"Well, I didn't. I'm a nobody from two working class parents. I'm carrying on the family tradition. So far in my life my biggest adventure was getting on this cruise liner to start a new career. Then I met Adam and we had an amazing romantic evening together that escalated into this bizarre proposal. My first reaction was to say no, but something inside told me to do it. I haven't traveled. I haven't dined in five-star restaurants or even had a reason to buy a cocktail dress. I'm not here for Adam's money, I simply want an adventure. I want to live a life that is so unlike my own, it will feel like being in a dream. Even if it only lasts for two weeks, I'll still remember it my whole life." Zoe picked up her glass and sipped her wine as the rest of us sat back impressed with her answer.

Then just as I was about to comment, I felt a hand on my shoulder.

"Good evening, boys. Do you have space for one more?" Elaina stood above me dressed in a silk cream dress. She stood there proud of herself, knowing that every man in the room was watching her.

"Oh, Elaina." I got up and turned around so that she could see Zoe. "I'm sure we can get the waiter to squeeze another chair round the table, but first, let me introduce you to my girlfriend." I reached out my hand for Zoe to take it. She put her hand in mine and stood up. "Elaina, this is Zoe. Zoe, Elaina."

Zoe took Elaina's hand and shook it while Elaina froze in shock. "It's so good to meet you. I've heard so many things about you from these guys... all good of course." Zoe played her part perfectly while everyone around the table watched the drama unfold.

"Oh, your girlfriend... I, I didn't realize..." Elaina stuttered, trying to get her words out and everyone was amused watching her squirm under the pressure. Elaina looked Zoe up and down. She wasn't happy to see another attractive woman at the table and it completely threw her off track.

"You're more than welcome to join us." Zoe rested her hand on my arm as she leaned in. "Adam, why don't you offer Elaina your chair while we get the waiter?"

"No! No. There's no need for that. I just wanted to stop by and say hello again to you all." Elaina looked across at the table of old friends in complete embarrassment. "I don't want to interrupt your meal. I have plans of my own that I probably should be getting to." Elaina started to walk away as Zoe shouted after her.

"It was nice to meet you!" Elaina waved back as she disappeared through the tables and out of the restaurant. Zoe and I sat back down as the whole table erupted into laughter.

"It worked!" Loukas shouted first as the others joined in. "I can't believe it actually worked!" They all continued to laugh and make comments about how rattled Elaina looked as I gazed over at Zoe. Who was this stunning woman, suddenly confident and willing to fight for me? I was in awe of her brilliance and completely captivated by her charm.

CHAPTER 11

Zoe

The next morning when I woke up, I went into the kitchenette for coffee. I found a note next to the coffee pot from Adam. "Gone to the gym, will be back for lunch."

I stretched lazily then pulled the sash on my robe a little tighter. This had been one of my conditions in agreeing to his plan, that I be moved to a room bigger than a closet. In fact, Adam agreed right away given that it wouldn't work for me to be staying in the crew quarters. I was given a small suite just a few doors down from Adam's.

I might have been a little old fashioned, but I didn't have any intention of sleeping with anyone I wasn't married to so moving into Adam's suite wasn't an option. Believe me, every time he looked at me with his smoldering dark eyes, my mind went to intimate places I shouldn't be thinking of. But I truly was committed to my standards. I half expected Adam to insist I move in with him, but he didn't. I was relieved to not have to argue because besides the obvious, I needed some boundaries.

The one thing I did give in on was having keys to each

other's suites for convenience purposes. It must have been convenient for him to slip into my room and leave a note. I let out a breath of nervousness at the thought of being in a closed suite with him while I slept. Knowing I had to get hold of myself, I went to get ready for the day.

Having showered and dressed, I decided to take a stroll out on the deck and enjoy the morning sunshine before I was back on 'fake girlfriend' duty. As I closed the door to my suite, I felt a hand tap me on the shoulder.

"Zoe! I was just thinking about you! My, what a coincidence!" Elaina appeared out of nowhere dressed in a white blouse and flowing black silk pants.

"Elaina? What are you doing here?" I was startled by her unexpected presence and tried to compose myself.

"I'm just on my way to the spa. Why don't you join me?" She leaned in as I tried to move away down the corridor.

"No thank you." I didn't know what to do. It felt too early to be mixed up in the game that was intensifying way too fast.

"Have you ever had a hot stone massage? Oh, they are just divine. Far too heavenly and relaxing to pass up. I simply won't take no for an answer." She slipped her arm around mine and started walking me down the corridor. "This will give us girls time to catch up. I want to hear everything about you and Adam! I'm sure he's told you all about me since I'm old friends with all the guys."

I desperately tried to think of something so that I could get away from her. "I should really go tell Adam where I'll be."

"Oh, you're a grown woman. I'm sure you don't need to tell him everything. We'll pop down to the spa, have our treatments, and then a little breakfast. You'll be back before he even notices you've gone." She held on tightly to my arm and I knew there was no way I was going to get out of it. I yielded to her will and decided that it might be a good opportunity to find out more about her.

We headed down to the spa and were immediately ushered into a room, no questions asked. It was then that I realized the whole thing was a setup. Elaina had already prepared them for our arrival.

"Please undress here and then lie down on the table. Your masseuse will be with you shortly." The lady pointed over toward two massage beds and then walked out of the room.

"Um, are we not in separate rooms?" I looked over at Elaina and she was already undressing.

"Of course not. We're going to be side by side, then we can have a good chat." She pulled down her pants and threw them onto the bench. She was wearing lacy red underwear which she started to peel off. I didn't know where to look and started pulling at my own clothes. I was so unprepared for this moment. Not only was I wearing mismatched under-wear, but I was standing beside a Grecian goddess that looked amazing, dressed or naked. And honestly, I was so uncomfortable with her lack of inhibitions it felt even worse to be me at that moment.

Confidently, she walked off to the table and lay down. She pulled the sheet over her backside which I was more than thankful for. I followed behind like a sheep being led to slaughter, not knowing what was about to happen. I lay there, facedown, with my cheeks squashed into the gap waiting for something to happen. Eventually, two ladies entered, and they started to place large hot stones on my back.

"Mmmm. Doesn't that feel amazing, Zoe?" Elaina sounded like she was enjoying herself while I just felt uncomfortable. All I wanted was to be somewhere else. Any other place than where Elaina Panagos was.

"Oh, yeah. It's great." I lied through my teeth as I wondered why anyone thought this was relaxing.

"So, what do you do for work, Zoe?" The first question came, and I knew it wasn't going to be the last.

"I'm a makeup artist." I kept telling myself to keep it simple. I wasn't the best liar, so I tried to tell the truth when I could and not overembellish.

"Wow, that's so interesting. I love makeup. In fact, my first starter company was a little online makeup boutique. Perhaps you've heard of it – Glam?" I already wanted to throw a hot stone at Elaina's head and we'd only got through the first question.

"Glam, really? That's amazing. I use their stuff all the time. I didn't realize you started it." Of course, I'd heard of Glam. It was the fastest growing makeup brand in North America.

"I helped get it off the ground. I sold my interest years ago, but I hear it's still growing. I'm not a pro with makeup though. I just play around with it really; you'll have to give me some professional tips." She was making her point loud and clear that I was a nobody in comparison to herself.

"Um, sure. Anytime." Elaina was frustratingly beautiful and probably didn't need to wear much makeup at all.

"Is that how you met Adam? Were you doing the makeup at an event he was attending?" Just another comment to dig at the fact that I was common in comparison to Adam. I hesitated for a second not knowing how to answer. I hadn't discussed with Adam our 'how we met' story. It really was a very basic question and something we should have covered.

"Yeah, exactly." I tried not to add any detail so that if the story came up again, I could always say she misunderstood.

"Adam has always been charitable with his time – was it a fashion show or charitable event?" That was it, I couldn't carry on with the torture. I was losing my mind while slowly being burned to death all at the same time.

"I'm sorry. I think I'm done with the massage." I turned slightly and waved at the lady standing next to me to take off the stones. She quickly obliged as I could hear Elaina shouting out in the background. "I'm sorry Elaina, this just isn't really my thing." I wrapped the towel around my body and jumped off the table. I grabbed my clothes and rushed into a changing room. By the time I came back out, Elaina was already fully dressed, waiting for me in the lobby.

"Darling, are you okay? I've been standing here frantic, wondering if you're all right?" Elaina rushed over to me pretending to be concerned.

"I'm fine. I just don't think lumps of hot rocks burning my skin are my thing." I tried my best to keep cool and not let her know that it was her incessant questioning that had tipped me over the edge.

"I suppose it's not for everyone. I love it, but I have very particular tastes." She looked at me like I was a peasant. "Let's go get something to eat. They have a lovely little terrace area where we can have some brunch."

I didn't have the energy to argue with her and I was starving. I followed behind her as she led me out to a secluded pool that must have just been for spa customers. We sat at a table and quickly had drinks and all kinds of nibbles brought out to us.

"I guess you're wondering why I'm even on the cruise? It's probably a little unsettling to know Adam's ex-girlfriend is on vacation with you." She looked at me like I was a bug and I knew this was the time not to show any reaction.

"Not really. Adam explained that you're meeting his parents for business. It's nice that you all get to catch up, as you haven't seen them in a while." I gave the best answer I could think of as she watched me. She smiled an unsettling grin that made me feel vulnerable.

"Zoe." Elaina sat up and leaned across the table. "You seem like a nice girl, a little naive, but nice. So, I'm going to be completely honest with you. I'm not here on a business trip to meet Adam's parents. I'm here to get him back." She looked at me square in the face, unflinching.

"Oh? Well, then. Um, but, wasn't it Adam's parents who invited you on the trip?" I wasn't surprised by her honesty, I just wanted to understand who initiated the plot.

"Oh, they told me about the trip, and it was their idea for me to gatecrash your vacation, but I made the mistake of letting Adam go once before and I'm not going to make that mistake again. So I hope you understand you don't have a chance. You see Zoe, you just don't belong in our world."

"There's only one world, Elaina." Now she was just starting to annoy me. It was one thing for her to go after Adam, but another to insult me.

"That's sweet." She smirked as she leaned back in her chair. "You see, Adam's parents know that he should be with someone like me. Someone successful; well-educated, cultured, and with all the right connections. I am Adam's equal and I know what makes him tick. You on the other hand, what can you offer him that he can't get from any other common girl at a bar?"

I wanted to lunge across the table and rip her pretty long hair from her head. Who did she think she was?

"I think we're done here, Elaina." I threw my napkin down onto the table as I raised to my feet. "You know, I gave you the benefit of the doubt against all my good judgment. I thought, let's just give her a chance, but I should have listened to my gut instinct. You might think you're perfect for Adam, but he's with me. I'm sure if you're as amazing as you think you are, you'll be able to find your own boyfriend."

"I hope you're up for a fight!" Elaina shouted out to me as I walked away enraged.

I marched myself back through the deck and into the main lobby of the ship. The halls were buzzing with families and people looking for activities as I stormed by. I knew Adam and I were just playing pretend, but Elaina's attack felt personal. She didn't think I was good enough to be with him simply because I didn't have her wealth or family connections. Elaina didn't know me. She didn't know my character or heart, but she had judged me according to her high class standards. And it was true. Using Elaina's ranking, I had nothing, and I was a nobody. Did I really think that someone as interesting and as wealthy as Adam would fall in love with me? How would I be able to hold his interest when I had nothing to offer?

Her words started to twist my thoughts as I raced down the hallway and into my suite. Adam was sitting alone on the sofa reading a magazine when I charged in and rushed into the bedroom. It was a little dramatic, but I could already feel the tears flooding my eyes. I was so upset it didn't even dawn on me to wonder why he was in my rooms instead of his own.

"Zoe?" I ran past him and dived onto the bed knowing that he would follow me in. "Zoe, what's wrong?"

He stood there in the doorway as I looked at him with watery eyes. "I was just with Elaina." That's all I could get out before the tears started to pour down.

"What happened? What did she say to make you upset?" He came and sat beside me as I cried.

"She accosted me this morning as soon as I came out of the room and forced me to go to the spa with her. I didn't know what else to do, so I went. She had the whole thing planned out already with hot stone massages in the same room. How embarrassing! She undressed right in front of me, and then started asking me questions about us. I just wasn't prepared for it. Then at the end, she basically said I wasn't good enough for you—that you should be with someone like her. Well, she actually said you should be with her, not me." I sobbed my way through the story all the while Adam held my hand.

"I'm so sorry, Zoe. I had no idea she was going to do that. It's my fault, I shouldn't have left you." Adam leaned down and started to softly kiss my fingers.

"She said she's here for you. It's not about business at all. She's come here to get you back." Adam didn't seem surprised by the revelation. Apparently he knew Elaina was capable of something just like this latest stunt.

"Ignore everything she said to you. In her mind this is all a game and she'll say anything to upset you. I won't leave you alone with her again, I promise." He continued to stroke my hand and gently kiss my fingers. It felt amazing and I wanted to give in to my senses, but I couldn't.

"I don't know if I can do this, Adam. It's one thing to play your girlfriend at dinner, but I don't like all this confrontation. I don't like how small and insignificant she makes me feel." I couldn't help but be honest. Elaina was beautiful, successful, and intelligent, everything that any man would want.

"She is nothing compared to you, Zoe. She might have money and prestige, but what type of person is she? She's cruel and calculating." Adam kissed my hand again and then he looked at me with his large round chocolate eyes. "You're a million times the woman she is. I just want you." He leaned in and kissed my lips and I couldn't help but give in. I kissed back and felt the electricity surge between us.

Right then and there I wanted nothing more than to have this fairy tale come true.

CHAPTER 12

Zoe

Our final days on the cruise liner passed in a blur of activities spent with Adam and Abby. After my altercation with Elaina, Adam decided that we would spend minimal time separated so that Elaina couldn't corner us. In the evenings, we mainly dined inside our room, by ordering in and only ventured to the 'safe' family friendly restaurants that Elaina wouldn't want to go to.

Adam would invite his friends to join us and we would normally all end up back at Adam's suite either playing games or watching movies. It felt that I had become an honorary member of the group and they had all eventually warmed up to me. Even Silas and Zach, who had originally doubted me, now happily talked openly with me. I felt welcome and part of the group which was more than a great feeling.

Abby was loving all the extra time she was having with her father. Most of our day would be spent down by the Kids Zone where she would occupy herself on the bouncy castles, slides, and the large swimming pool. We had become our own family unit in the space of a couple of days.

"Zoe, can we go on the surfboard today?" Abby jumped up onto my lap as I read a magazine on the sofa.

"Surfboard?" I looked at her puzzled, wondering if she was confused about going to the beach.

"Yeah. Up on the top deck they have a surfboard that you can ride. If you fall off, you fall into the pool. It looks like fun." She picked up a piece of my hair and twiddled it in her fingers.

"Oh, the simulator. I don't know honey. You'll have to ask your dad." Just as I answered, Adam came walking out of his bedroom.

"Daddy, can we go on the surfboard today?" Adam turned and gave the same confused look that I had made only a moment earlier.

"There's a simulator up on the top deck." I filled in the missing bit of information.

"Um, I don't know, Abby. Don't you want to go down to the Kids Zone like we normally do?" I could see Adam was concerned about going somewhere so open in case we bumped into Elaina.

"No, I want to go on the surfboard. I'm bored with staying in the Kids Zone." Abby looked at her father with wide eyes.

"I'm not sure if you're old enough to go on the simulator. It might be just for big kids." Adam stood with his hands on his waist as he thought about it, but I knew he was fighting a losing battle.

"Oh please, Daddy. This is our last day and I really want to go on the surfboard before we go." Abby gave her best sad face, but it was obvious that she'd already won Adam over.

"Well, I guess as it's our last day it would be fun to do something different." Abby jumped up and down, excited.

"Zoe, do you want to skip this and chill out here? Or you could soak in the tub in your room." I knew he was only thinking about me avoiding Elaina, but I didn't want to miss out on the fun either.

"Nope. Zoe has to come. We all have to go on the surf-board. Everyone is coming, Natalie and Uncle Silas, too. Everyone!" Abby pulled at my hand for me to sit up and I was glad that she had answered for me.

"I guess we're all going!" I smiled at Adam as I stood. "Let me just run down and change into my swimsuit and then we can head out. I'll be right back." I headed for the door with my fingers crossed that this spontaneous event would go off without any snags.

"Sure, I'll call the guys." Within twenty minutes, we'd all gathered at the top deck around the simulator. Unfortunately, with it being the last day, everyone on the ship had the same idea. The whole deck was packed with families and people lining up for a go on the surfboard.

"This is insane! Are you sure you want to hang out here?" Zach looked over at Adam as we huddled together.

"It's what Abby wants to do on the last day. You guys don't have to stay, I can wait in line with her." Adam looked up at Abby who was seated on his shoulders and enjoying her view above everyone.

"No way, we all have to do this. I want to see you fall flat on your back!" Loukas laughed as he tickled Abby's bare foot.

"Can't you use your power to get us to the front of the line? We're going to be here for hours!" Zach turned to Loukas and thought it was about time he used his authority for something useful.

"I don't know if that's a good idea, man. If we push past everyone and jump the line, we might have a mob on our hands." Loukas wasn't shy about using his position, but it probably wouldn't help them on this occasion.

"Loukas is right. They'd kill us if we jumped the line. We're just going to have to wait our turn like everyone else." Silas added his thoughts as we all looked over at the huge line. Then suddenly a familiar voice came out of nowhere.

"I didn't realize you were all so cowardly." In unison, we all turned to find Elaina standing beside us. As we stared, she took off a thin scarf to reveal a bright red bikini. "Here, hold this." Without hesitation, she handed Loukas her bag and then marched off towards the simulator.

The whole group watched as she made her way through the crowd unphased by anyone's comments. She swished her hips and flashed her smile at the perfect moments, using her feminine charm to make her way to the front of the line. I could feel myself getting angry but also feeling completely powerless as every man on the deck watched Elaina. Adam, our group, and every man in the place was watching her curvaceous figure in that tiny red bikini. We all stared as she leaned in and spoke to the man in charge of the simulator. She laughed and he smiled back, ignoring the crowd of bodies before him. Then she suddenly pointed over to our little group in the distance and he handed her a microphone.

"I'm sorry to interrupt your fun, everyone." Elaina could suddenly be heard across the whole deck and everyone watched in silence. "But it's a special little girl's birthday today and her one wish is to have a ride on the simulator. Do you mind if we let my very good friend Abby have a ride? She turns five today!" Elaina pointed over to Abby and Adam as the whole crowd turned and smiled at them. "Can we all say Happy Birthday to Abby?" The crowd erupted into clapping and shouts of celebration. "Get yourself up here and enjoy your birthday ride!"

Under the pressure of every eye in the place watching them, Adam made his way forward with Abby still sitting on his shoulders. We all watched as the line let them pass through. Adam helped Abby onto the surf simulator, and everyone cheered as she took her ride. I watched enraged as Elaina smiled and laughed beside Adam. She would touch his arm as they watched Abby together and it made my blood boil.

"I can't believe Elaina just did that. She made it look so simple." I stood with Loukas, Zach, Silas, and Tanner as they all commented on how impressed they were with Elaina. It wasn't long before Abby fell off the surfboard into the water and the whole crowd cheered. Adam helped to fish her out and within a few minutes they were back in our huddle with Elaina.

"Elaina, that was amazing!" Loukas couldn't help but pour out praise.

"Well, a little white lie never hurt anyone." She looked down at Abby and squeezed her cheeks with her hand. "I know it's not your birthday, but I couldn't let you leave without having a ride on the simulator."

"Thank you, Elaina." Abby looked up and she was also clearly impressed with Elaina's beauty and ability.

I stood silent watching the whole thing unfold before me. Were we still playing pretend or was the game over and I just didn't realize? I tried to look at Adam to signal that we should go, but he was lost in conversation with Silas. Everyone was caught up in their own conversations, mainly about Elaina. I stepped back and wondered if anyone would notice if I just left, so I did. I walked away, leaving them all on the deck feeling completely defeated by Elaina and her supernatural powers in a red bikini.

An hour later, there was a knock at my door. I'd had a shower and my hair was clean and shiny. My sundress was nicely pressed and I felt a little better about how I looked compared to Elaina, the amazing power woman. Whe I hoped the door, Adam stood there looking confused. "Hey, what happened to you? One minute you were there and the next you were gone?" I didn't even look up to answer him and just continued throwing my clothes into my suitcase. "Zoe?"

"How long?" That's all I said as he walked over to the bed.

"How long what?" He sounded frustrated, but I didn't care. I was frustrated, I was sick of this silly game. A scheme I should never have agreed to in the first place.

"How long did it take you to realize I was gone?" I looked him straight in the face and I could see his hesitation.

"Zoe, why are you so upset?" He reached out his hand and touched my arm. I pulled away, not wanting to be drawn in by his touch.

"Why am I upset? I guess I should have brought my little red bikini or better yet, I should just walk around in my underwear. That seems to be the only way to get your attention." I was mad, mainly at Elaina, but I let my frustration out on Adam.

"Wait a second, that's not fair. I didn't know Elaina was going to be up there, and I didn't know what she was going to do."

"Why did you ask me to do this... to be your girlfriend, if you were just going to play right into her hands as soon as she walked around in a tiny little bikini and did something fairly obnoxious to help your daughter jump a long line? Are you really that distracted by appearance, that you'll forget everything for a busty bimbo?" I may have pushed too far, but I couldn't get the image of everyone drooling over her out of my mind.

"Hey! I took Abby on the ride because she was desperate to go on it. What did you want me to do? Say 'No thanks, I'll wait' when she was given a free pass? I didn't even speak to Elaina. I came right here as soon as I realized you left. Now

94

do you want to calm down and tell me what this is really about?"

He stood beside me, unflinching and all I wanted to do was collapse into his arms. I'd worked myself up beyond my own understanding and now I just wished I could take it all back. I looked like a jealous, foolish child just because I couldn't cope with Elaina's stunt. I sat down on the bed and held my hands up in frustration.

"It's just too much, Adam. I don't know how to process all of this. One minute it's just us and Abby, and everything is wonderful. I love being with you and seeing you play with Abby. But then I'm suddenly aware that it's all a game and I need to be defending myself against Elaina. I just didn't realize how hard this was going to be and it's really just an act."

Adam sat down beside me and put his arm around my shoulder. "Maybe this wasn't the best idea. I had hoped that Elaina would back off when she saw I had a girlfriend. I didn't think it would make her more determined. I'm really sorry. We can stop all this. You don't have to do this anymore." He held my hand and I wondered what it would mean if we did stop. Would I stay on the ship and never see him again? Would I be able to get my job back? "I just want you to know that I've really enjoyed our time together. It hasn't felt like we've been pretending."

"I don't want this to end, but I just don't want to pretend anymore. I'm not silly enough to think I can take it when I can't." I looked at him, completely physically and mentally exhausted by all the drama.

"Okay then. Let's promise that we won't pretend when we are with each other. The ship docks tomorrow and we'll have two days before Loukas's birthday party. Why don't we go away, the three of us, and see if this really works? I can show you where I grew up and there's some amazing sites to see.

Just give me the next two days and then if you want to leave, I won't stop you. I know that's not much time, but it's really all we've got right now."

As he looked down at me with his arm still around my shoulder, I felt safe. I didn't want to see any more of Elaina, but I knew I wasn't ready to say goodbye to Adam. What difference was two more days in the grand scheme of things?

"Okay. I'd really like to see where you grew up." I smiled up at him hoping this wasn't the biggest mistake of my life.

CHAPTER 13

Adam

"This trip was meant to be a group vacation. The pact, remember? Now you're flying off for two days?" Silas looked at me like I'd betrayed him.

"I'm not going to spend the next few days arguing with our parents and being harassed by Elaina. This is my vacation too." We stood on the dock beside the huge cruise liner which was now almost empty as its inhabitants were out exploring Mykonos. The rest of the guys had all taken a car up to my parents' villa, all except Zach who was waiting for Silas inside their own hired car.

"I just thought you'd want to use this time to reconnect with Mom and Dad, not go off with some woman you've just met." I could see that Silas was irritated, but it wasn't my job to babysit him. He would be fine hanging out with the guys for a few days without me.

"Hey, Zoe helped me out a lot with the whole Elaina thing. There's no need to be rude about her. You have your opinions and I respect that, but I won't have you speaking ill of her." I looked off to the side where Zoe and Abby were waiting for me in our own hired car.

"I'm sorry. I like Zoe, I just don't see why you need to disappear. Can't you just come to the villa with us?"

"Stop acting like a baby." I slapped him playfully on the shoulder as I turned to leave. "I'll be back in time for your big bash. I'm sure Loukas has plenty of crazy things planned for you all while I'm gone. Have fun, little brother." I waved him goodbye as I headed over to the car. Zoe jumped out to put one last case into the trunk.

"Everything okay?" She raked her golden hair back and smiled.

"Everything's fine. Silas is just a little sore that we're leaving. He'll get over it." Now that we were leaving the ship, I could see that Zoe had relaxed. She seemed more like herself and I was looking forward to spending time with her and Abby alone.

"Are you sure you don't want to bring Natalie along?" Zoe got into the car as she asked her question.

"No, I told her she can have a few days off. I think it'll be fun just the three of us." I slammed the door and turned to look at Abby. "Right, monkey?" She giggled as I turned back around and reversed the car. As I looked in my rearview mirror, I could see Elaina standing alone on the dock with several large cases. I breathed out a sigh of relief knowing that I wouldn't be seeing her again for a few days.

The first day was a blur of driving around Mykonos showing Zoe and Abby where I went to school, hung out with my friends, and generally spent most of my time. It was all just as I remembered with its stone whitewashed buildings and cobbled streets. We sat at a café in the town square and sipped on cappuccinos as we watched locals and tourists go about their business.

"I can't believe you grew up here." Zoe looked around, amazed at the beauty of the local town square. "It's like permanently being inside a postcard. You must think everywhere else is grey and dull in comparison." She looked at me, expecting me to have the same reaction to its beauty.

"It is beautiful. Coming back, I can see that more now, but for me, it holds too many memories. A place can be tainted by bad memories which affects how you view it." I looked out onto the square and saw a young family walking by with a baby in a stroller.

"What do you mean, tainted?" Abby stopped eating her ice cream and looked up at me confused. I reached across the table and picked up my drink.

"Well, you're enjoying your lovely ice cream, but if I poured some of my cappuccino into it, the whole thing would be spoiled. Wouldn't it?" Abby nodded as she watched my cup hover above her bowl. "It's the same thing. When you look out over this square, you see the beautiful buildings, the terra-cotta tiles, and the locals enjoying themselves. I see my ten-year-old self standing alone in the center of the square singing a Christmas carol against my will because my parents forced me to be in a Christmas concert. I wasn't a very good singer and I was so nervous that I almost threw up." Abby giggled as Zoe listened to me. "My father is a great singer and he expected the same from me, but I wasn't good. I hated all the attention and everyone in my school was there. They all pointed and laughed at me, so I ran away. My mother was furious. She said I had embarrassed the whole family and as punishment I didn't get any Christmas presents that year."

"No Christmas presents?" Abby looked at me gobsmacked. She couldn't comprehend a Christmas without presents.

"Wow, that's a pretty harsh punishment for something that wasn't even your fault." Zoe looked at me with sympathy. It was one of those old wounds that had never healed from childhood.

"Well, there are worse things in life than not getting Christmas presents." I looked back over the square still remembering that cold Christmas night when I was laughed off the stage as a child. Zoe reached her hand across the table and rested it on top of mine.

"Don't just brush off your childhood pain like it doesn't matter. You've overcome it and you're not that little ten-year-old boy anymore. But the hurts don't cease to exist because you got over them." She smiled at me as I tried to process what she was saying. Don't we all still feel like children when we're with our parents?

"Why don't we go to the beach? I know where there are some really cool caves I know you'll love." I poked Abby in the belly and quickly moved on from the subject. I didn't want to dwell too long on past pain, especially not with Abby around.

We finished our drinks and headed off to the beach which was only a short drive from the town center. Abby was in her element, running along the sandy shore and kicking her feet in the cold sea water. Zoe and I walked along side by side, barefoot, feeling the warm sand between our toes.

"Can I ask you a question?" Zoe paused as we watched Abby off in the distance enjoying herself.

"Sure." I didn't know what she was going to ask me, but she sounded serious.

"It's a personal question and you don't have to answer. You told me that your wife died, but you didn't tell me how she died. I just thought maybe I should know as I'm pretending to be your long-term girlfriend." I could see she was apprehensive about asking me and I didn't realize that I'd never told her.

"Of course, you can know. I honestly assumed I'd told you." I looked down at my feet and thought about the terrible night my wife died. "It was a car accident. I was at home with Abby and Megan was driving back from a girls' weekend. It was her first trip away with her friends since we'd had Abby. She was hit by a drunk driver. He didn't wait at the stop sign and went straight through into her side of the car."

"Oh, that's awful. I'm so sorry." I couldn't bring myself to look up at Zoe, knowing that she'd have the sorrowful sad eyes I received all the time as a widower.

"Yeah. Nothing really prepares you for that. You think your life is going well and then everything falls apart because one person didn't stop at a stop sign. She was so good with Abby and since she's been gone I've made a strong connection with my daughter. I'm not sure that would have happened if Megan had still been here. I'd probably have let her do most of the parenting without realizing how much I was missing out on. That has to be the silver lining I was meant to take from it, I guess." I looked back at Abby with tears in my eyes thinking about how she was blissfully asleep when her mother died.

"I haven't ever dealt with loss like that, so I'm sorry I don't have the words to comfort you." Zoe laced her fingers into mine and I appreciated her refreshing honesty.

"It's fine. There's really nothing anyone can say. It happened and now we're learning how to move forward."

"Thank you for sharing with me. I just think it's amazing that you've been able to bring yourself back from that and raise Abby. She's such a lovely little girl. You should be proud." Zoe meant every word of what she said, but I could tell that there was a deep sadness behind her words. She looked away down the beach and I could see that she was lost in her own thoughts. It wasn't just my sorrow that troubled her.

"What is it?" Zoe turned back to me with watery eyes.

"I'm sorry. You're going to think I'm very selfish. You've just told me about Megan and all I can think about is my own pain." She wiped away a tear from her eye and she was clearly ashamed of whatever she was thinking.

"You don't need to apologize for that. What's troubling you?"

"It's just that this whole experience has been a little overwhelming for me. Not just because of Elaina, but because I've gotten to know you and Abby so well." Zoe looked down at the ground unable to look at me for some reason. "The thing is… I can't have children." She swallowed and looked up to the sky fighting back tears. "I think it's what led Alex to cheat on me. I couldn't give him a family and he stayed with me because we were already married, but eventually it became this big unspoken thing between us. It ate away at us until there was no more reason for us to be together. So, you see, being around Abby has been a little overwhelming."

"I'm so sorry Zoe, I had no idea. I wouldn't have pushed you into this, into spending time with us if I'd known." I felt awful hearing that my daughter was a point of pain for Zoe.

"No, no. Abby is wonderful. I love being with her and truthfully, it's actually been a very healing experience for me. I thought it would be painful. I thought she would just remind me of everything I can't have, but I've been very inspired by you both. The way you have both overcome losing Megan and continued to live is just amazing."

Abby smiled up at me and I couldn't bear to see the admiration in her eyes. She looked at me like I was a hero, but I was anything except a hero. I hadn't overcome the pain of losing Megan. I had hidden away, distanced myself from my friends, and was only on the vacation because they forced me into it.

"I'm not inspiring, Zoe. Abby might be, but certainly not me. I've had some pretty dark times since Megan passed and I wouldn't exactly say I'm through the woods." I could still see Abby splashing in the water and I knew she was the only reason I had kept living.

"I'm not saying it was easy, Adam. It was dark and messy and very, very painful, but you kept going for Abby. And no matter how broken you may feel, that really is inspiring. I didn't lose anybody to death; I simply had a cheating husband and I almost gave up entirely. I'm ashamed of how lost I let myself become." Zoe slumped her shoulders and I pulled her into myself.

"Don't do that. Don't disqualify your pain or compare it to mine." I raised her chin up with my finger and looked into her glassy blue eyes. "You've been through loss, it's just a different kind. You're allowed to grieve. You're allowed to mourn for the loss of your marriage and for the child you can't have. Let yourself feel it, because that's how you'll get through it." I couldn't believe the words were coming out of my mouth. I could hear myself saying things to Zoe that had been said to me and I hadn't believed them. I was trying to console her when I couldn't even face my own pain.

Zoe stared at me with her watery eyes and quivering lips. "I'm scared this is all going to end."

I could see the fear in her eyes, and I didn't know how to answer her. I didn't want to lie by promising her the world, but at the same time I felt the same wonder about where this was heading. Instead of replying, I pressed my lips down onto hers and firmly kissed her. We were two broken souls clinging to hope. The hope of a happy future potentially in each other's arms. For now, hope was enough.

CHAPTER 14

Zoe

The two days we had together passed by too quickly. When Adam turned the car into his parents' drive, I could already feel the knots in my stomach twisting. I wanted to reach across, grab the steering wheel, and shout, "No, take us back to the beach!" We had been safe at the beach in our threesome. We'd shared ourselves openly on the sandy shore and enjoyed our time playing with Abby. Why couldn't we stay there? Why did we have to end something that had been so perfect?

"My family's villa is just up the hill." Adam pointed up to the top of the rocky hill where the road twisted and bended all the way to the top. I could just barely make out the white walls of a building, but it was too far off to see it clearly.

"Wow, that's high up. Are you sure when we get to the top we're not going to be greeted by St. Paul and the pearly gates?" Adam chuckled at my joke, but I was genuinely terrified by whatever waited for us at the top of the hill.

"Is this where you grew up?" The car slowed as we made our way further up the hill.

"Yeah. My family has lived here for generations. It started out as a small shepherd's hut generations ago but has now grown into a huge complex. My parents still call it a villa, but it's really much more than that."

"This must have been quite the commute to school." I looked back down the hill and could feel my stomach fluttering. I wasn't normally scared of heights, but the narrow roads and sharp bends were making me feel sick.

"Ha! You could say that." Adam smiled, amused by my comments. The car finally took its last turn and we drove into a huge open driveway with a large water fountain in the middle. Adam pulled the car up to a large set of cream marble steps. A young man dressed in a white uniform suddenly appeared and took the keys from Adam without question.

"There's a valet?" I'd never seen anything like it. I couldn't even think of a restaurant I'd been to back home that had a valet. This really was another world and another reality.

"Yep. You'll get used to it. My parents have a lot of help in the house." Adam answered like it was nothing as he helped Abby out of the car.

"Wow Daddy, your house is enormous!" Abby looked how I felt, completely stunned by the grand entrance. Rather than arriving at someone's house, it felt like arriving at a five-star resort with a huge open hallway and elaborately decorated columns.

"This is Grandpa and Grandma's house, not mine." Adam reached his hand out to his daughter and smiled at her as she put her smaller one in his. We walked into the main entrance hall to be greeted by a butler.

"Welcome, Master Adam. Your parents are waiting for you in the courtyard." Adam slapped the aged butler on the arm as he walked past, which wasn't appreciated.

"It's good to see you again, Philip." He winked at me as we

carried on through the house. Everywhere I turned there were gold vases, marble statues, and the shiniest floor I'd ever seen. It was how I imagined Madonna or Elton John living, not my boyfriend's family.

I followed Adam as he led us through a large set of glass doors into a courtyard that was surrounded by balconies on every side. The courtyard had a very different feeling to the grand entrance hall. The walls were still a natural pink brick color and green vines grew between the pillars of the balconies above. A large curved pool was the center feature of the space and I could see Loukas and some of the guys passing a volleyball back and forth. As we walked out, everyone stopped and all the guys in the pool gave a cheer at our arrival.

"Adam, you're finally here!" A tall slim woman in her fifties walked over, dressed in an entirely cream outfit. Gold bangles and chains decorated her arms and neck. She opened her arms wide as she walked across the courtyard. Without even looking at me, she kissed Adam on both cheeks and then quickly turned her attention to Abby. "And this must be my granddaughter. Oh, how delighted I am to finally meet you, darling." She bent down and hugged Abby for a few seconds.

"Mother." Adam immediately stiffened and I was surprised by how quickly his mannerisms changed. "This is my girlfriend, Zoe Ross."

With my whole body shaking, I stepped forward and reached out my hand, expecting her to shake it. "It's so nice to meet you, Mrs. Nicolis." She looked down at my hand and then glanced at my face.

"Charmed." Without even flinching, she took Abby's hand and led her away over to Mr. Nicolis. "Come, Abby. Come and meet your grandpa!"

I stood there feeling out of place and quickly put my hand

back down as Adam gently put his hand on the small of my back. I had never met anyone so rude and for a few seconds I was so flustered I didn't know what to do.

"You finally made it then!" Silas rushed over, still dripping wet from the pool. "We weren't sure if you would turn up or not." He smiled at Adam and then leaned in to brush his wet cheek against mine.

"Yeah, starting to regret it already." Adam wasn't ignorant of his mother's cold welcome, but it was too late, we were already in the lion's den.

"Oh, relax. Mom has talked about you the whole time. She's been desperate to see you, she's just got her guard up, that's all." Silas waved absently at his parents across the way and shook his head. "Why don't you come join us in the pool? We're playing volleyball."

"Thanks, but I should probably go say hi to the old man and save Abby." Silas headed back to the pool as we made our way over to his dad. Abby was sitting on her grandfather's lap, being asked all sort of questions about school and her life in New York.

"Hey, Dad." Adam stood there and smiled as I remained beside him awkwardly. His father lifted his head to acknowledge that he'd seen Adam but continued to talk to Abby. "And do you have any pets in your fancy apartment in New York?"

"No. I keep asking Daddy if I can have a puppy, but he says they need too much attention." Abby was already at ease chatting away to her grandparents.

"You should get her a dog, Adam. It's good for children to look after animals. It teaches them responsibility." Adam's mom looked up at him and I could see from his face that he was irritated. He hadn't been here longer than five minutes and he was already getting orders about how he should look after his daughter—the grandchild they'd never met until just now.

"Abby, why don't we go find your room. A nap would probably do you good." Abby looked up at Adam, sad that she was already being pulled away from her grandparents.

"I have your room all made up. I had it decorated especially for you, and you just let me know if you need anything." Adam's mom took Abby's hand and started leading her back into the main part of the house.

"I'm just going to put Abby to bed. I'll be back soon." Adam started to walk away, and I felt completely abandoned. I was glad that his parents had gone off with him, but I didn't want to be left alone with the guys and Elaina. I turned and watched them all playing volleyball for a few minutes wondering what I should do with myself, but I wasn't alone for long.

Elaina had been sitting on a lounge chair sunning herself while watching everything that happened. As soon as she saw me alone, she came over, eager to mix things up.

"Hello Zoe." Elaina was wearing a white swimsuit and a pair of white linen pants. She always looked refined and annoyingly perfect.

"Elaina." I sat down at one of the round iron tables wishing she would leave me alone.

"Did you enjoy your trip around Mykonos? It's a beautiful place, isn't it?" Elaina sat down opposite me and crossed her legs over.

"Yep, it's pretty spectacular." I was intentionally keeping my answers short, not wanting to give her any unneeded information.

"It must be very different from where you grew up. My family actually has a villa not far from here. My family is very close with Adam's. You see, we know all the same people."

"No red bikini today?" I couldn't help but make a comment as she was trying to upset me. Elaina smirked, knowing I was referring to her antics on the cruise liner.

"Not today. It's always helpful to have something like that in your wardrobe, you never know when it might be needed." Every word that came out of her mouth annoyed me.

"I prefer to use my brain rather than my body to get what I want." I didn't see the point in being civil with her when we both knew that we disliked each other.

"And how's that working out for you?"

"Well, I'm here with Adam… so, I'd say it's going pretty well." I couldn't help but be smug about being with Adam when I knew she'd do anything to get rid of me.

"Yes, but for how long? Do you really think your relationship is going to last long when he sees how out of place you are here? He might find it charming now that you're bewildered by all this wealth, but that will quickly fade when he realizes you have nothing to offer him." Elaina leaned in over the table and narrowed her eyes on me. "Adam is a man of the world with a huge appetite. He needs a woman that understands his world and can keep him entertained. Once he's had his fun with you, he'll simply move on to somebody more suitable."

"You mean somebody like you?" I glared back at her, trying to hold my nerve together.

"We all know he should be with me. His parents know it. His friends are thinking it and deep down, I think you know it too. You won't ever be accepted here; it's just best you know it now." Elaina stood up and looked over at the guys in the pool. "Enjoy the few days you have here, I can't imagine you'll ever be coming back." She stood up, smirked, and then walked off back to the pool. I wanted to lunge at her. To smack her across the face or rip her hair out. How dare she talk to me like that?

I watched enraged as she slipped out of her pants and stepped into the pool with the guys. They welcomed her into the game without hesitation and Elaina immediately started hitting the ball and making jibes at the guys. She was confident about her place in the group, in this house and with Adam. I wanted to run away, but I had nowhere to go. I didn't know my way around the villa, and I couldn't run out the front door and sulk like a child. No, I had to sit there and watch Elaina edge me out of the place I'd suddenly realized I really wanted to be.

But maybe Elaina was right? I had never seen wealth like this before. Of course I'd known it existed somewhere, but I'd never been able to fully understand what it looked like. These people were accustomed to the finer things in life in every single area of their life. They lived a champagne lifestyle, full of glamourous parties, friends, and luxuries. I couldn't compare that to my life. I collected coupons at the grocery store and mended holes in my jeans with patches. I didn't know anything about how to manage a company or be successful in business. And apparently, I'd made a bonehead decision to leave a good job to come on an adventure that would leave me broken hearted and feeling like a shabby chic girl next door.

I sat quietly alone and thought about how crazy that was. When I'd been waiting on the dock with my parents to board the cruise, I had been so excited about starting my new career. Getting on the ship and starting a new job had been a big step forward and then I'd given it all up so easily. Part of me wished I could go back to that moment and not get on the cruise liner so that I could avoid being where I am now. As I lost myself in thought, Adam suddenly appeared at the table. He pulled out a chair and sat down without saying anything. We sat in silence for a moment when he finally looked at me.

"Are you okay?" I asked lowly, even though I knew the answer before I got his response.

Adam's expression was as furious as I felt. He bit his bottom lip and clenched his fist as he sat there brooding.

"I'm fine." His tone was sharp and direct. He clearly wasn't fine and obviously didn't want to talk about it—at least not here and now.

I looked away wondering how we'd both ended up so upset within the space of about an hour. We'd been happy on the drive here, cracking jokes and messing around with Abby, but now we were anything but happy. Our happiness had been sucked dry and replaced with anger and bitterness as we settled into our own separate cocoons.

CHAPTER 15

Adam

I could tell from the moment I walked into the courtyard and saw my mother sizing up Zoe that this was going to be a difficult week. You would think, after not seeing my parents for over ten years that they would be eager to embrace their son and get to know him again. That they would show some type of emotion toward me, but no, I don't receive a hug or any warmth at all. Nothing. All of my mother's attention went straight to Abby, which is understandable, but I would have thought they would at least hug me. Something, anything to let me know they'd missed me and still loved me. My father couldn't even be bothered to get out of his chair.

It's one thing for them to be rude to me, but Zoe doesn't deserve it. My mother was cold and sharp with her. I could see Elaina sitting in the background and she had undoubtedly given them the skinny on my non-Greek girlfriend. I purposely arrived late so that we wouldn't have to spend a whole day with them and when I suggested taking Abby for a nap, I hadn't expected my parents to come with us.

"I have Abby set up in the yellow room. Well, it used to be

yellow, but I had redecorated pink for your visit." My mother led the way into Abby's room which looked like a unicorn and Barbie had planned the decor. The walls were a hideous candy pink and the bed, chairs, and tables were covered in pillows, throws, and anything else fluffy or with ruffles that my mother could find.

"Do you like your room, Abby?" My mother stood back and admired her handiwork as Abby looked around in amazement.

"It's amazing." She walked around the room looking at all the toys and gifts that had been left for her.

"I have stuffed animals lined up there and of course they're all yours. You can choose one to snuggle with for your nap. There are pajamas in the top drawer for you when it's bed time." My mom was gushing over all the surprises for my daughter and it was getting to be a little much.

The door suddenly opened behind us and my father walked in. "Did you have to bring that woman with you?" He didn't waste any time getting straight to the point.

"Excuse me? Do you mean my girlfriend?" My dad stood in the doorway with his arms folded. He had aged since the last time I saw him. His hair had greyed and the wrinkles in his face had deepened. I had always been scared of my dad. He had a low gravelly voice that instilled fear and would fly off into a rage at any moment. Despite the fact that I was now an adult, he still terrified me.

"I don't care what you call her, she shouldn't be here." Abby froze and looked up at us both. "She's not welcome."

"I'd rather not talk about it in front of my daughter." My dad might have been willing to argue in front of Abby, but I wasn't.

"Abby, let's get you snuggled down for a short little nap. You want the turtle to have a nap, too?"

Abby nodded and climbed onto the bed and curled up.

My mother covered her with a pink hand crocheted blanket and brushed her hair back.

I leaned down and kissed my daughter's forehead. "Sweet dreams. I'll see you soon, my love."

My mother signaled for us to go out and we all walked out into the hallway. I pulled the door closed behind me and put my hands on my hips ready for the assault my parents were ready to launch.

"Why have you brought her here, Adam?" My mother immediately started the inquisition with no preamble or warm up.

"Are you serious? She's my girlfriend, why wouldn't I bring her here? And more to the point – what is Elaina doing here?" It didn't seem to matter that we'd left Abby's room as our voices were still raised.

"Elaina is a family friend. Of course, she would be here to celebrate Loukas's birthday." My mother stood straight, willing to fight for her side.

"Oh, she's just here for the birthday party, is she? Then why was she mysteriously ended up on the same cruise as us? And she couldn't keep her mouth shut about how you want to bring her into the business. Does Silas know that he's being replaced by Elaina?"

"Don't be ridiculous. Elaina isn't replacing anybody." My father looked over at my mother, waiting to see if she would reveal the full plan.

"Well, what's she doing here? I haven't seen her since college and I'm truly okay with her absence in my life. I didn't realize we were inviting everyone's ex-girlfriends to family celebrations these days. When did that start? And why can't you just stay out of my business?" I could hear in my voice that I was getting worked up and I think I was starting to let all of my frustration out.

"Adam, you were happy with Elaina. I remember how

upset you were when you two broke up. She's still single and you're single again, so there's still a chance for you to be together." My mother looked up at me hopefully, but I didn't believe she was concerned about my happiness.

"I don't want to be with Elaina. You might think she's amazing simply because she's Greek, but she's only interested in me because of your fortune. She has absolutely no interest in me as a person. And I'm with Zoe now. Zoe is the perfect match for me." I was already getting tired of explaining myself and couldn't believe we had gotten into an argument so quickly.

"And who is this Zoe person? Some makeup artist from New York? That's not a serious career. How can you be with someone like that?" I looked at my father, completely disgusted by his comment.

"Not everyone owns successful hotels. Not everyone comes from money, you know. There's nothing wrong with having to work. I work and manage to survive without your help." I looked down at the ground, wishing I could just disappear.

"I just can't believe you brought her here. She has nothing to offer you, I just don't understand it. She's not Greek, she has no education or culture. I mean, what do you see in her?" My mother looked at me genuinely confused and a wave of pity came over me. I was so thankful that I didn't think like either of my parents. They lived their lives constantly judging people by their own narrow standards, and I could see how pathetic it was.

"She's a human being, Mom. I see the person she is, not what she has or doesn't have. And she is educated, she used to be a school teacher but changed careers. She's amazing with Abby and she happens to be one of the loveliest people I've ever met."

"She stopped being a teacher to become a makeup artist? Oh my." My mother raised her hand to her mouth in shock.

"That's seriously the only thing you heard from all I said? You're unbelievable." I turned to walk away but then had one last surge of rage take over me. "I haven't seen either of you for over ten years. You didn't come to my wedding to Megan because she wasn't good enough for me. You didn't come to see Abby when she was born because her mother was beneath you, and you didn't come when Megan died. You have absolutely no right to be interfering in my life when you've shown no interest in it before. If you want me to stay this week and if you want to see your granddaughter, I'm warning you to stay out of my life and to leave Zoe alone." Fed up with their nonsense, I walked back down the hallway to the courtyard.

"This is amazing! I've never seen anything like this before!" Zoe looked out across the beach and couldn't believe all the festivities that had been set up for Loukas's birthday. A large section of golden beach had been cordoned off for our private party and it was filled with volleyball nets, elaborate sandcastles, buffet tables, and large white tents.

"It's pretty impressive." I was surprised myself at the expense the family had gone to for the day celebrations considering there was still an evening reception to come.

The long-anticipated day of Loukas's birthday had finally arrived and he was in full form welcoming guests to the beach. We'd had a difficult couple of days staying at my parents' house and had tried our best to either stay with the group or go for long walks just to avoid them. It was difficult as they constantly wanted to spend time with Abby, but I was also concerned that they would indoctrinate her to their way of thinking. Abby already had a privileged life back in New York, I didn't want her to become even more spoiled by the constant attention she was receiving.

"Look Daddy, there's a bouncy castle." Abby pointed over to an enormous yellow and blue bouncy castle that had different sections and water slides.

"Oh my. I know what you want to do first!" I winked at her and we all walked over.

"Hey! Isn't this something?" Loukas spotted us on our way over and stopped to say hello.

"It certainly is. Did you know all this was happening?" I gestured my arms to encompass the whole beach.

"I only knew about tonight's party. I had no idea my parents had arranged all this. I think your parents had a lot to do with it too." Of course, they did. They wouldn't pass up an opportunity to show off their wealth.

"Well, happy thirtieth birthday! I don't think you'll be able to beat this birthday." I patted Loukas on the back and watched as Abby jumped into the bouncy castle and disappeared.

"We're going to start a volleyball tournament in a minute. You guys have got to be in it." Loukas looked at Zoe and me, excited by the prospect of playing in the tournament.

"Um, I think we might give that a miss and just hang out with Abby." I looked down at Zoe and tried to read her expression. I wasn't interested in competing and assumed that it wouldn't be something she'd want to do either.

"I'm not taking no for an answer. It's my birthday, you all have to do as I say!" Loukas started to walk away over to the volleyball area. "Head over this way and we'll get started."

I rolled my eyes and gave out a sigh. "I don't think we have much choice."

"That's okay. We'll play one game, get knocked out, and then we can enjoy the rest of our day." Zoe smiled up at me as I appreciated her logical answer. She was dressed in a pair of red linen shorts and a silk white vest top that moved in the breeze. She looked effortlessly beautiful and I was so thankful for her presence that past few days. Being with my parents was stressful, but we had the added stress of Elaina always watching us and making snide comments.

"I know it's been difficult, but I just wanted to say I really appreciate you being here. It's made a huge difference." I squeezed her hand as she looked up at me. "Now let's go lose our game of volleyball."

We headed over to a single wooden table that was situated beside the volleyball area. Loukas had made himself the boss and was ordering people around. A large wooden chalkboard was behind him and he'd drawn up a grid showing all the matches and the knock-out rounds.

"Right! Ladies and gentlemen, welcome to my birthday celebration volleyball tournament! You've all been divided up into couples and you'll find your partner written next to your name on the board. To make it interesting, I've rearranged people from their natural partners, and I don't want to hear any complaining! Let the games begin!!" Loukas threw his arms up into the air and the crowd cheered.

"Can you see our names? I can't see who I'm with?" Zoe stood up on her tippy toes to look at the board. I looked over and spotted her name.

"You're with Silas."

"Oh." She slumped down and looked at me with disappointment. "Who are you with?"

I searched for my name and finally found it near the bottom, but I couldn't believe who Loukas had paired me with.

"Elaina." I looked around for Loukas who had mysteriously disappeared. "I'll change it. I'm not playing with her, don't worry."

"Hey, partner." Then just as I turned to find Loukas, Elaina suddenly appeared. "You ready to play?" She smiled at me, but I could see the smugness in her eyes. She was thrilled that we'd been put together and wasn't afraid to show it.

"I need to find Loukas. I'm not being your partner."

"Come on, Adam. It's just a game. Surely Zoe can live without you just for the tournament." Elaina turned to Zoe and flicked back her long brown hair. "I promise I won't steal him."

I looked down at Zoe expecting some type of reaction, but she calmly stared back at Elaina. "It's fine, you guys can be a team. I wouldn't count on winning though. Silas and I are going to beat everyone." Zoe turned to me and then unexpectedly kissed me hard and firmly so that Elaina could see. "Have fun."

Zoe turned and walked away, leaving me with Elaina. I was completely stunned by her kiss and wanted more.

CHAPTER 16

Zoe

When Elaina walked over all smug because she was paired up with Adam for the volleyball tournament, something inside me took over. I wasn't going to shy away or freak out like I did on the cruise, this time I was going to fight. A hidden competitive streak within me took over and I could tell that I had surprised Adam. He looked dumbfounded when I kissed him and walked away. It was just the confidence boost I needed as I headed into the tournament with Silas.

"So, we got paired up. You any good at volleyball?" Silas smiled at me, assuming that I'd have no skill with a volleyball.

"I played a little in high school." I thought I'd wait and let him see me in action before I told him volleyball was my main hobby and sport throughout my adolescence. I'd even played intramurals in college. So, I wasn't concerned about my abilities with volleyball.

"Great, so I don't need to explain the rules. I think we're playing Loukas and Tanner first." Silas stood next to me in only a pair of dark navy shorts. He had a similar look to Adam, being brothers, but he seemed a tad more conceited about himself. "It might be easier if you hang back and let me do most of the work." He smiled and it was clear he was used to getting what he wanted all of the time.

"Whatever you say, boss." I played it coy and waited until we started our first game with the hope that I might be able to 'accidentally' hit him in the head with the ball.

The tournament started and our first game against Loukas and Tanner went off without any problems. They passed the ball back and forth to each other without trying to get any serious hard hits in. Loukas wasn't paying too much attention as he was more concerned with who was watching them rather than playing the game. Tanner also wasn't exactly a volleyball man and simply tried his best to keep up with the game.

"Are you trying to let them win?" After ten minutes of continued back and forth without any major points, I decided to intervene.

"You're welcome to take over!" Silas gave me a sharp look, assuming that I was complaining about his volleyball skills.

"Sure, let's switch." Confused by my sudden boldness, Silas moved and on the next serve I punched the ball hard into the opposition's side and scored a point.

"I didn't know you could play like that!" Silas smiled as he put his hands on his hips.

"Like I said, I played a little in school." I smirked as I looked over at Loukas and Tanner. "Are you girls going to pass the ball or just stand around admiring yourselves?"

Loukas swung around and gave me a huge smile. "Where did this spitfire come from? Have you been hiding all this time, Zoe?" He hit the ball and within the next pass I'd scored another point. "Hey, you know you have to let the birthday boy win, right?"

"The fact that you suck has nothing to do with your birthday and frankly, it isn't my problem." Now that we were on a winning streak, my confidence grew and I could easily trash talk and enjoy the fun.

Loukas and Tanner tried their best to score some points, but within a few short rounds, Silas and I had won and were moving on to our next match. Loukas took losing well and quickly switched his attention to being the commentator for the final games.

Our next match was against Zachary and another relative that I'd never met before. Silas and I played well together and by the end of the game we'd gotten ourselves into a familiar rhythm. Our last match was the final and unsurprisingly we came up against Adam and Elaina.

"You better get ready for a beating, bro; your girlfriend is a pro at volleyball." Silas shouted over to Adam who was standing on the other side of the net.

"So, I hear!" Adam looked at me and winked. His skin was glistening from the sweat and he looked every bit the Greek god as he stood panting in the sunlight. For a moment I forgot my motivation and just watched Adam.

"You won't be able to beat the dream team!" Elaina put her arm around Adam's shoulder and leaned her head into him. She looked at me as she held him, but Adam quickly moved away and gave her a disagreeable stare. My motivation was back – I wanted to lay Elaina flat on her back. I was going to beat them, even if it meant beating Adam too. There was no way Elaina and Adam would be crowned the volleyball champions, not if I had anything to do with it.

"Ladies and gentlemen, we have come to the final game of the tournament and what a game it is. We have brother against brother and lover against lover! Adam and Silas go head to head with their respective partners, Elaina and Zoe. Adam is teamed up with a college friend while Silas is teamed with Adam's girlfriend. If this game had any more drama, we'd be watching a Greek tragedy!" The crowd laughed as Loukas shouted out his introduction. Adam stood with his hand on his hips, unimpressed with Loukas's summation while Elaina waved and blew kisses to the crowd.

"Don't forget, whoever gets crowned the volleyball champions not only wins a gold cup, but they also get to dance the first dance at my birthday ball later this evening. Players, are you ready?" We all gave a quiet shout back. "I said— players, are you ready?" We all shouted louder and this time the crowd cheered along with us. Loukas blew a whistle and then we started.

The first few rounds were very intense with us both scoring points in equal turns. Surprisingly, Elaina was also very good at volleyball and Adam could hold his own. Silas and I played well together but we didn't have enough skill to completely destroy them. I tried hard not to look at Adam as I didn't want to get distracted and instead I focused my attention on Elaina.

"The game is neck and neck. There's only one more round left. It all rests on this final round!"

Elaina hit the ball into the air, and it came directly at me. I jumped up and hit it, but as I landed, my ankle gave way and I fell down onto the sand. I gave out a little cry of pain as I fell and within seconds Adam was by my side asking if I was okay.

"Did you hurt yourself?" He looked down and lifted my foot into his hands.

"I just twisted my ankle. That's all." He turned my foot in his hand to see if it was broken. I could feel a sharp shooting pain, but I couldn't give up.

"With only one serve left, this injury couldn't come at a more unfortunate time. Silas and Zoe are ahead by two points. If they win this final serve, the game is theirs. But if they retire from the game now, they forfeit, and Adam and Elaina will win. Zoe, are you able to continue?" The crowd went quiet as Loukas came and stood over me.

"You don't have to do this, Zoe. It's just a game." Adam looked down at me, concerned but behind him I could still see Elaina. She was still on her side of the net but as she spotted me looking at her, she raised her arms and mimicked a baby crying. She was mocking me.

"I can play." With a final surge of energy, I pulled myself up onto both feet even though my ankle was burning. I took the ball out of Loukas's hands and marched painfully over to my position.

"And she's back in the game!" The crowd cheered as I took my place. "This is the final serve... let's see who will be crowned the Volleyball King and Queen!!" Loukas blew his whistle and as it echoed through my ears, I threw the ball up into the air and hit it as hard as I could aiming for Elaina. The ball flew through the air and hit her smack in the middle of her stomach. The crowd cheered as the ball hit the ground and Elaina went down to her knees.

"Zoe and Silas are the volleyball champions. Please give a huge cheer for your new King and Queen!!!" Loukas rushed over and handed us a huge gold cup which we both held in one hand. It was a small victory, but I felt like a true queen. Adam smiled at me and clapped while Elaina stormed off in a rage.

The rest of the day passed in a blur of beach activities and sunshine until it was time for the evening event. Loukas had organized a grand ball to be held at the Nicolis flagship hotel, The Golden Olive. All the stops had been pulled out to make the affair as luxurious and elaborate as possible. Everyone had been instructed to dress only in white or navy blue and gold masquerade masks were handed out.

Thankfully, the only formal dress I had packed under my mother's instructions was a silk deep blue ball gown. I could still hear her voice as I pulled it out of my case, "You never know if you'll end up attending a ball or dance on the cruise liner. You'll be glad you packed it then!" I certainly was glad and as I slipped into it, I felt like a million dollars. It had thin strips that rounded my shoulders leaving the back completely open. I could hear the bass of the music bumping from down in the ballroom and knew the party was already underway. Adam had left me in my room to get ready while he took Abby down for a quick dance before it was her bedtime.

I pinned back some of my blonde hair so I could put on my mask and when I looked in the mirror, I was surprised to see a sophisticated lady looking back at me. I smiled to myself and counted my blessings. Here I was in Mykonos staying at one of the most luxurious hotels in the world and about to attend a fancy ball with the sinfully gorgeous Adam Nicolis. In that moment, I didn't care that our relationship was on uncertain ground. There could be a budding romance between us, or it could still be just pretend, but either way, tonight was going to be magical and I'd remember it forever.

After spritzing on some perfume, I made my way down to the reception hall. The lights were dimmed low and the whole room was packed full of people dancing in the ball-room or sitting at tables. I spotted Abby and Natalie dancing, but no Adam. Then out of the corner of my eye I saw a group of people huddled in the corner. I made my way over and realized it was Adam talking with his parents. His hands were moving in an animated fashion and they all looked like they were in the middle of a heated debate.

"How many times do I have to tell you that I don't care!" I

could hear Adam's voice and decided to hang back. I didn't want to interrupt them if they were in the middle of a family discussion.

"How can you not care? She's not Greek! She has no heritage, no connection to your homeland, and no reason to treasure your family roots." Adam's mother shouted back.

"Why does it matter? Megan wasn't Greek. I don't even live in Greece. You really need to get over this weird obsession about everyone being Greek." I stood in my place not knowing if I should listen or not. They were clearly talking about me and I wanted to know what Adam's parents really thought.

"Abby is precisely why you need a Greek wife. She needs to grow up knowing where she comes from, surrounded by family. You should be living here with us, not with strangers in New York." Adam's dad started waving his hand around and pointing his finger.

"I can't believe you two! I'm a grown man with my own life. You can't tell me where I should be living and who I should be dating, and you especially can't tell me how to raise my daughter. Abby's mother was American and she's going to know that side of her heritage."

"Really? And do you think Zoe is going to encourage that? She doesn't have children. She's a failed teacher and a divorcee who's likely only with you because you're her meal ticket out of her pathetic life." Mrs. Nicolis didn't hold back her real feelings and as I heard every word come out of her mouth, it was like a dagger repeatedly stabbing me. I was a failure. I couldn't have children. I was a divorcee and a gold digger.

As her words soaked into my mind, another voice whispered into my ear. "See, I told you that you'd never be welcome here." I turned to find Elaina standing next to me watching the whole conversation. She was dressed in a pure white silk gown that almost looked bridal. "Adam could be happy in Greece with his family. Abby could know her grandparents, but you're holding them back. You're depriving him and Abby of their family simply because you think you're in love. Love doesn't solve everything. Eventually Adam will regret leaving Greece and he'll regret staying in New York for you. You'll become a noose around his neck that he'll do anything he can to get rid of you. It's best to accept your relationship is doomed now and save yourself the heartache." I pulled down my mask and looked at Elaina with watery eyes. I'd never met anyone so cruel.

Adam suddenly spotted us and rushed over as I turned to walk back out. "What did you say to her?"

"Only the truth." I heard Elaina's smug remark as I started to run. I couldn't be there any longer, not with his parents, not with Elaina and her poison. Tears started to pour down my face as I ran out of the ballroom.

CHAPTER 17

Adam

I chased Zoe all the way through the ballroom, pushing past people and desperately trying to catch up to her. By the time I finally broke through the crowd, she had already made it into the elevator and disappeared. When I made it back to our floor, I was flustered, sweaty, and prayed that she was still there.

"Zoe?" I knocked on her door and was relieved when I realized the door wasn't latched. Normally, I'd have been annoyed that she'd been careless and unsafe, but this gave me a chance to talk to her. I pushed the door open and didn't immediately see her, but I heard crying coming from the bedroom. When I turned the corner and stepped into the bedroom, Zoe lifted her head up and looked at me. Her black mascara was smeared down her cheeks and her beautiful silk dress was tearstained.

"Oh, Zoe. What did Elaina say to you?" I rushed over and sat down next to her on the bed.

"Nothing that isn't true." Her words were mixed in with sobbing and for a few minutes she cried uncontrollably as I rocked her in my arms. I was heartbroken for her but at the same time completely livid with Elaina. She'd obviously said something truly vicious for Zoe to break down like this. Eventually she calmed down and her breathing started to slow.

"You shouldn't believe anything Elaina says. She's just twisted and bitter." I lifted Zoe's face and tried to dry her cheeks with the cuff of my shirt. Her face was blotchy and pink but her blue eyes still sparkled.

"It's not just Elaina, Adam." Zoe moved away and sat upright as she pulled her hair back from her face. "I heard what your parents were saying about me. That I'm a failure, a divorcee, and not Greek." She sniffed and wiped her nose with a tissue as I sat in shock. "Oh, yes, and I'm a gold digger to boot."

I didn't realize that she'd heard our conversation and was understandably upset by what she heard. I was horrified myself to hear their true thoughts, but not surprised.

"I don't know what to say, Zoe. I'm sorry you heard any of it, but... but that's not what I think at all. I'm not them." I leaned back to look into her eyes. I needed her to see the sincerity of what I needed to say to her. "You aren't a failure and I couldn't care less that you're divorced or that you're not Greek. If anything, that's a plus in my book. My parents are determined to control me and that makes them very, very judgmental. Wealth, prestige, and notoriety has made them pompous, arrogant people who think money is the key to everything. But they can't buy me, and they can't tell me what to do. It drives them mad and this is how they lash out. None of what they said was true and it was all directed at me, not you."

Zoe remained silent as she looked down at the floor thinking through everything I was saying. "I should never have asked you to come on this trip and pretend to be my girlfriend. I should have asked you from day one to just *be* my girlfriend." Zoe lifted her head in surprise and gazed at me. "I know this has been far from ideal, but I have loved spending every moment with you. Your smile, your laugh, your witty little jokes... everything about you makes me happy and I don't want this to end. I want us to officially be together, and I don't care what anyone thinks or says."

Every word was true, and it felt freeing to finally tell Zoe how I really felt. For the past two weeks, we'd been trying to not rush our relationship, to keep things easy while we played this game, but things had been far from easy. The only relief I'd had during this vacation was spending time with Zoe and Abby. She came into my life like a breath of fresh air and I wasn't ready to let her go.

"You really feel that way? You're not just saying it to make me feel better?" Zoe held her gaze on me and I could see the hope seeping back into her face.

"I mean every word Zoe. You're everything I want. We can leave right now if you want and go back to New York. We can go home and start out fresh with a clean slate. We can pretend like none of this ugliness ever happened." When I first started talking, I could see a spark in her eye light up at the thought of us being together, but halfway through my speech, I could see her attention drift. The hope faded from her eyes and she turned away.

"No, we can't do that." She kept her head down and slumped her shoulders over in defeat.

"Yes, we can. We can leave right now and head straight to the airport or we can go in the morning. No one will stop us." I looked at her confused, wondering why she was rejecting my offer.

"We can't pretend like none of this happened because it matters. It matters to your parents, to Abby, and to all of your friends down there. I'm not saying Elaina is completely right, but she's not entirely wrong either." I couldn't believe what Zoe was saying. Only a few hours ago, she'd been crowned the Volleyball Queen and had taken great pride in beating Elaina even with a twisted ankle, but now she was freely giving up. "I want to be with you Adam, I really do. There's something real between us, something I haven't felt for a long time, but I can't pretend like it's perfect. I don't belong in your world and eventually you'll come to see that too."

"No. No, that's not true. There aren't different worlds, just the one we can create together. Please, don't throw this away just because of what Elaina said." I clutched onto her hand and desperately wanted to make her feel how much I needed her.

Zoe raised her hand and rested it gently on the side of my face. "For us to be together, you have to choose between me or your family. I'm not going to let anyone pick me over their family, no matter how much I love them."

I could feel warm tears filling my eyes as she looked at me. Zoe had told me she loved me at the same time she told me she was leaving me. I could feel my heart breaking and it wasn't until that moment that I realized how much I had come to love her. The realization hit me hard – it had happened fast and unexpectedly, but it was real.

"But I already left my family. I live in New York and I hardly speak to them. This isn't a difficult choice for me to make. Please Zoe, don't do this… there has to be another way. It's not a black or white issue." Zoe stood up and now it was me falling to pieces.

"You have a chance to mend things with your family. Abby should have a relationship with all her grandparents, and she should know that she has a rich Greek heritage. I'm not going to take that away from her so that we can be together." Zoe paused, looked at the door, and then turned back to me. "I'll leave tomorrow and find my way back home. This isn't how I wanted our vacation to end, but I think it's the best. Please don't track me down in the morning... please just let me go."

With that, I released Zoe's hand from my grip and I quietly walked from her room.

CHAPTER 18

Adam

"Do you want some coffee?" Natalie looked over at me as I sat at my work desk.

"No thanks." I looked back down at my laptop as though I was in the middle of something important but really, I was just gazing into space. That's what I'd been doing the past hour instead of answering emails and making work calls. I'd been back in New York for three weeks since returning from Mykonos and I just couldn't get back into the swing of things. My productivity was practically zero and I was just fortunate that my team was fully capable of running without me and had not yet realized my complete lack of effort.

Natalie frowned at me and I could feel her judgment. She'd seen the change in me since we had returned from vacation and although I tried to hide it around Abby, Natalie could see that I wasn't the same. I tried to engage in conversation with her, but I just wasn't interested. It wasn't just Natalie; I wasn't interested in anything anyone had to say. All I could think about was Zoe. My mind swirled with endless questions; what was Zoe doing now? Did she return to be a makeup artist? Has she met someone new and forgotten me? I'd ponder these questions over and over and still find myself sitting aimlessly at my desk or looking out of the window.

I understood why Zoe broke things off with me, but it still hurt. We both wanted to be together, but my overbearing, closed minded family ruined everything. When I'd left Zoe's hotel room, I'd walked straight down to the ballroom and given Elaina a piece of my mind. I told her exactly what I thought of her and how there was no chance of us ever getting back together. And I meant *ever*. Nothing changed, I was still angry, still frustrated, and still heartbroken. Zoe had given me up so that I could keep my family, but it wasn't a family I wanted to keep—at least not the way they were.

"Adam." Natalie stood in the doorway of my office and I wondered if she'd been watching me the whole time.

"Um, yeah?"

"Zach's here. Do you want me to bring him back?" I sighed and stretched my arms out. I really wasn't in the mood to see anyone, but if he was here already it was unavoidable.

"No, I'll come and see him. Thanks." Natalie disappeared back down the hallway and I followed behind. Zach was sitting in the living area talking to Abby.

"But why can't we see Zoe?" Abby asked. Zach looked scared to answer and as he spotted me, he turned away from Abby and shrugged his shoulders.

"Abby, we've already talked about this. We won't be able to see Zoe anymore, okay?" Abby's little shoulders slumped down, and she hung her head. I hated being sharp with her, but I just couldn't answer her endless questions about Zoe's strange disappearance.

"Hey, why don't you go to the park with Natalie. I need to talk to your dad about something and when we're done, I'll come meet you in the park. Okay?" Zach winked at Abby and patted her on the top of her head.

"Good idea, I was just thinking we could do with getting out." Natalie walked over and took Abby by the hand. "Some fresh air will do us good." Abby looked at me as she walked away, and I could tell she was hurting. She missed Zoe, just like I did.

"Adam, what's up with you? You don't normally speak to Abby like that." As soon as the girls were gone, Zach wasted no time getting to the point of his visit. I sat myself down on the couch opposite him and tried to keep my cool.

"She just keeps asking about Zoe and I don't know what to tell her. I'm struggling to even know what to think myself." Zach looked at me and then he looked down at his hands.

"After Mykonos, I thought you'd come back and get over Zoe pretty quickly. I thought she was just a summer romance, your first fling since Megan, but I can see now that she meant a lot more to you than that."

"It wasn't a fling, Zach; we weren't even together in that way. I know you guys didn't see it, but we really clicked. And I'm frustrated about how we ended things." I knew that Zach had never fully warmed to Zoe, but that was only because he was overprotective of me and maybe still a little loyal to Megan.

"Then go find her. Change the story and win her back. You can't keep living in misery when you can do something about it." Zach looked at me and I could see the frustration in his eyes. He was tired of dealing with it. To be fair, throughout our friendship he'd put up with a lot and had seen me through the worst times in my life. Now, he just wanted to see me happy and he couldn't understand what was stopping that.

"It's not that simple. She told me to let her go – that she wouldn't be with me if it was going to break up my family." I gave a little chuckle as I thought about my parents back in Greece. "And what's funny about it all is that I don't even see my family. I've lost Zoe because of them and I don't even see them. They're still the same closed-minded people who haven't supported my choices."

"You never told me that was why she left. You just said it was over, I just assumed you had ended things." Zach looked at me with a puzzled expression while I couldn't even remember what I'd told the guys after Zoe left us in Mykonos.

"No, it wasn't me. I practically offered her my heart on a plate and said we could start over here, but she said no. She wanted Abby to have her wonderful grandparents and that wasn't going to happen if she stayed with me." I took a sip of my water and felt the cold liquid slip down, soothing my dry throat.

"And you let her go? I had no idea that she cared for you so much. You're right... we never saw any of that because we didn't spend that much time with the two of you together." Zach stood up as I stared at him in surprise. "Come on, Adam. You don't let someone like that go – you fight for them. If your family is the only reason that you're not together, then go and fix it. I'm not going to listen to you moan about your parents for the rest of my life when you can put on your big boy pants and go and sort it out." I was still sitting looking up in shock at Zach. "Get up!"

I stood up wondering why Zach had never spoken to me like this before or why I hadn't thought about doing this myself. "Go get your passport, jump on a plane and talk to your parents." Zach put both of his hands on my shoulders. "Don't take no for an answer from anyone."

"Adam, you're back so soon? Is Abby not with you?" My mother looked behind me hoping to hear Abby's little footsteps as she came into the main lobby to welcome me.

"No, it's just me." I kissed her on the cheek and smelled my mother's familiar scent. That hadn't changed in all the years since my childhood.

"Well, to what do we owe the pleasure of a second visit so quickly?"

"Is Father around? I need to speak with you both." It suddenly occurred to me that I should have called ahead to make sure that my father wasn't off on a work trip, but in my haste to get here I didn't think that far ahead.

"He's sitting in the courtyard reading. What's wrong? Abby?" My mother looked concerned, but I took her by the arm and started to lead her out into the courtyard.

"Nothing is wrong, I just need to talk to you." We stepped out into the glorious sunshine where my father had his feet up reading the newspaper.

"Adam has come to see us." My father lowered the paper and looked over at us through his narrow glasses.

"Adam?" He immediately stood up and again I was met with a concerned expression.

"Here, let's sit down." I pointed over to a round table beside me where there were enough chairs for the three of us to sit. I could see my parents looking at each other as they took their seats.

"It occurred to me recently that we've never really had a proper discussion since I've been an adult. I thought it was time I tried to explain some of my life choices. Having some of my logic from my own point of view clarified might help you understand me a little more." I was met with complete silence as they looked at me like I'd lost my mind.

"You see, I was still pretty young when I decided not to take my place in the family business and I never really explained why I didn't want it. Looking back, I can see how my sudden exodus would have appeared ungrateful. That I was acting out like a spoiled child. You both always provided everything I needed. You raised me, gave me an excellent education, and offered me the world and I always did appreciate that... still do. I wanted to find my own way, though. I could see my whole life laid out before me... managing the hotels, marrying Elaina, living in a huge villa, and socializing with the cream of society. I would basically become you and there's nothing wrong with that, it's just not what I wanted. You put so much pressure on me to follow in your footsteps that I felt like I had no other choice but to go as far away as I could to see what kind of businessman I could become on my own."

My mother lifted her hand to her mouth, and I could see that she was getting emotional. I appreciated that they had managed to remain silent throughout my talk, but I still had more to say.

"Elaina was my first serious girlfriend and at one time I thought we'd get married. But it got really uncomplicated when I told her that I'd left the family business and was going to make it on my own. It quickly became apparent that she didn't love me at all. Elaina disappeared without explanation and moved on to the next rich kid at college when I shared my plans with her." I took a deep breath and my mother sighed.

She looked at me and tilted her head blinking back tears. I felt I was at least getting through to her and hoped my father would start understanding soon, too.

I cleared my throat and continue with my story. All of it had to be told. "You see Elaina was only interested in your fortune and she could only get it through me. When I closed the door she wanted to go through, she had to find another source to tap." I paused for a moment to let that bit of information sink in. After another deep breath, I moved on. "When I moved to New York, I met Megan and realized that I'd never really been in love with Elaina. Megan completed me, she was my everything, and losing her was the hardest thing I've ever had to go through. It was harder than leaving the family, harder than starting my own business from nothing, and harder than finding the courage to come and talk with you today."

Suddenly my mom reached across the table and took my hand. It was a small sign of affection, but it meant more to me than words could express. I curled my fingers around hers to draw more comfort from her and to also let her know I appreciated her support even though I had no idea at that point how deep that support would go.

"I was angry for a really long time with you both. You didn't come to my wedding and then you didn't come to see Abby when she was born. I just couldn't believe that you wouldn't want to meet my child simply because her mother wasn't Greek. And then when Megan died, you didn't come to her funeral." I paused and swallowed hard, trying to hold back tears. "I was devastated. How could you not come to her funeral?"

My mother leaned forward and squeezed my hand. "We did."

"What? I didn't see you. You weren't there." I shook my head in disbelief and thought it was cruel of them to make out like they had been there.

"We didn't want to cause you any extra stress or pain by just turning up at the funeral after all that time. We thought you'd think it was grandstanding. We went to the grave and we saw you all doing the burial ceremony and it broke us. We saw you holding Abby and you were surrounded by Megan's family and all these strangers that we didn't know. It was then that we realized how much we had lost and how far we were from getting you back." A single tear fell from my mother's face and landed on my hand.

"We wanted to go over to you, son. We just didn't think you'd want us there after we didn't go to the wedding. I was concerned that we'd cause a scene by upsetting you further and that was the last thing we wanted to do. The hardest thing we ever did was walk away that day. We wanted to help you and to see Abby, but we just didn't think you wanted us there." My dad offered a sympathetic smile as we all clutched at each other's hands. We'd all been so isolated for years, thinking the worst of each other when in reality we just wanted to be together.

Not communicating had been our downfall. I was hoping that now was the end of that for all of us—Zoe included.

CHAPTER 19

Adam

After a long emotional night, the next morning I went for a walk on the beach to clear my head. It was a crisp fresh morning and the sand was still cold from the night before. The sun had only just started to break in the sky and warm the air. I walked along the waterside, feeling like a new man. I'd held on to so much anger and bitterness toward my parents that I now felt a hundred times lighter without it. The icy sea water lapped at my toes and awakened my senses. After so many years of being away from my family and ignoring my Greek heritage, it finally felt good to be home and know that I was welcome.

"Adam!" I suddenly heard my father's voice behind me.

"Dad?" I was surprised to see him up so early and on the beach. He had a very strict routine of working out, eating breakfast, and checking emails that he usually stuck to religiously.

"I saw you heading out. Do you mind if I walk with you?" It was a welcome visit, one that had never happened before.

"Sure. The water's pretty cold, but it's refreshing."

"I think I'll stay on the sandy side. I'm too old for ice cold water first thing in the morning." He smiled at me as we started to stroll side by side.

"I'm glad you're here actually, there's something I'd like to get your advice on." I had talked through everything with my parents last night, except the main reason of my visit… Zoe.

"Let me guess, it's about that young American girl you brought with you last time." I looked over wondering how he knew what I wanted to talk about as he playfully slapped me on the back. "I knew you were holding something back last night."

"I know you guys aren't fond of Zoe, but she's actually what motivated me to come here to sort things out with you and Mom. She broke up with me because she didn't want to be a wedge between us. The night of the ball she told me that Abby deserved to have a relationship with her grandparents, and she wouldn't be the reason that couldn't happen. So she broke things off and I haven't seen her since." I laid my cards on the table, holding nothing back so that my dad would know Zoe's real character.

"I see." He looked down at his feet and we both paused for a moment.

"I want to be with Zoe, but this time I want to do it the right way. I don't want us all to be holding onto issues from the past that don't matter anymore. I want you and Mom to be in my life and to know Abby, but I also want Zoe to be a part of that and to feel welcome. Do you think you guys can get over it that she's not Greek?" I wasn't sure how my dad was going to respond, and I could feel my heart pounding as I waited for his response.

"Your mother has demanded that you marry a Greek girl all these years in the hope that it will make you stay here. We don't care about having a pure Greek family – your mother's father is from Italy, for goodness sake. She just took that stand hoping you'd marry a nice girl from town and live nearby."

"Wow, are you serious? That did not work out the way she hoped at all!" I couldn't believe after all their years of Greek indoctrination, it was just a tactic to keep us close.

"Well, that's how it works with children. The more you hold on to them, the more they want to leave. You will find out soon enough when Abby grows up." My father smiled as we continued walking. "So, you're serious about this Zoe Ross?"

I was a little surprised that my dad remembered her full name. "I am. She's different from Megan but in a good way. She is funny and lighthearted and she's so affectionate with Abby."

"No one will ever take Megan's place, but it's good to hear that you're learning to love again. I want you to be happy and it's good for a man to have a wife. She obviously won't be Abby's mother, but again I'm sure she'll help Abby with the girly things that you don't know about." I smirked at my dad's traditional advice. He wasn't wrong, but it was still funny to hear him offer his thoughts.

"Do you think Mom will be okay with it?" I knew my mom would want us to move back to Greece now that we had reconciled but that wouldn't be possible if I wanted to be with Zoe.

"Hmmm. Your mother will put up a fight at first, but I'm sure if we remind her of what she has missed in the past then she will fall into line soon enough. She adores Abby and was heartbroken when you returned to New York, she won't want to miss out on any more of Abby's life." My dad slapped me on the back again but this time with more vigor. "Leave it to me. I'll talk to her."

"Thanks, Dad. I really appreciate it." We continued our

walk along the beach for a good hour, sharing stories from the past and our hopes for the future.

CHAPTER 20

Zoe

"Do you have some really thick concealer? My skin is atrocious!!" Hazel, a six-foot something model sat herself down in front of me.

"Don't be ridiculous, your skin is gorgeous." I reached across the table and picked up a liquid foundation bottle and started applying it to Hazel's face. Since I'd returned home from Mykonos, it had been a struggle to get any significant work and I had to get a job at a local beauty store in order to pay the bills. I still had most of the money Adam had paid me to pretend to be his girlfriend but I'd tucked that money away. I had no intention of using it unless I had no other option. Then out of the blue I got offered a job doing the makeup at a small fashion show for a new boutique. Thankfully, the show was on my day off and I was thrilled to be finally getting a professional gig.

"Is something wrong? You're pretty quiet for a makeup artist." Hazel looked straight at me as I gave her a fake smile.

"I'm fine, Hun, just thinking about what I'm doing." I started making small talk with her just to keep her from

147

asking any more questions. I didn't really want to explain to a stranger that I was brokenhearted. Nothing was the same since I'd returned from Greece. I'd seen a whole other world while I was on the cruise with Adam and during our stay at his parent's villa. I'd never seen wealth, luxury, or leisure like that before and it was disturbingly difficult to slip back into my old life. Everything seemed grey in comparison to my whirlwind romance and I couldn't shake it off.

It wasn't the loss of the rich lifestyle, the fabulous clothes, and fine dining that had me down… it was Adam. I missed him with all that I was. He'd seeped into my blood, become part of me, and I felt like a hollow shell without him. I thought I knew what love was, having been previously married to Alex, but now I realized I had never been truly loved or truly in love. Adam made me feel alive and not just with his crazy schemes and plans. He seemed to understand me like no other and I felt a natural ease around him. Leaving him was the hardest thing I'd done and over the past few weeks I'd been starting to wonder if it was the biggest mistake of my life.

"Oh my gosh! Tanner Lewis just walked in!" Hazel suddenly sat up in her chair and spun round to the opposite side. "It's him! It's really Tanner Lewis… I can't believe this." I could feel my heart pounding as I heard Hazel say Tanner's name, but I couldn't bring myself to look. If Tanner really was here, he'd recognize me and probably talk to me about Adam.

"Zoe?" I heard my name through the buzz of confusion around me and assumed it was Tanner. I could feel my confidence quickly fading and I knew I'd have to turn around and pretend to be happy. With my pulse racing, I turned to find Adam standing directly opposite me.

"Adam?" I couldn't believe it was him. I wanted to pinch myself and make sure I wasn't dreaming. He looked better than I remembered. Still tall, still dreamy, still drop-dead gorgeous. "What are you doing here?" Out of the corner of my eye, I saw Tanner in the background and then I realized this must be Tanner's fashion show.

"Don't be mad, but I asked Tanner to find you. He hired you for the show so I could see you." I stood there still in shock not knowing how to feel. I knew I should be annoyed that I had been hired for a pointless job, but I just didn't care with Adam standing before me.

"You wanted to see me?" Even though I was the one who had walked out on Adam, I had assumed that he'd been able to move on from me with ease. I hadn't expected someone with his abilities, wealth, and opportunity to miss someone like me. Believe me, I'd dreamed about him hunting me down but as the weeks passed I had come to accept that it wasn't going to happen.

"I've wanted to see you since the moment you left me in Mykonos. I've seen you in my dreams, I've thought about you every second and I tried as hard as I could to stay away, but you're part of me. You're the person I want to talk to when I wake up and the person I want to call when I have a problem. You're the only person Abby will talk about and my family is simply incomplete without you." Adam stepped forward and then got down on one knee. The whole room froze and went deadly silent as everyone watched in amazement. I held my breath in utter shock and wondered if I'd ever be able to breathe again.

"Zoe Ross. You have taught me the real importance of family and that above all, family matters most. For you, I have reconciled with my parents and I have even received their blessing to be here today and to ask you this very important question." Adam took out a blue Tiffany's box from his pocket and opened it to reveal a sparkling and utterly perfect diamond ring. "Will you be my wife and the missing part of my family?"

"Yes!" I couldn't get anything else out except my one-word acceptance. I completely forgot about the ring and flung myself into Adam's arms while the whole place erupted into cheers.

~

"Okay, have you got your basket of petals?" I looked over at Abby, dressed in a beautiful light pink gown with flowers braided into her hair.

"Yep." She lifted up her little wicker basket filled with white rose petals and smiled.

"Now are you sure you want this to happen? We don't have to do any of this. We could just have a big party and forget all about the wedding. What do you think?" I bent down and looked straight into Abby's eyes. I'd come to treasure this little girl more than anything in the world and I didn't want to upset her in any way.

Her little arm reached out and she wrapped her fingers around mine. "If you marry my daddy, does that mean I have to call you Mommy?"

I felt a chill down my spine as she asked me her simple question. My heart still longed for a child, but I'd never force my desire upon Abby. "No, you can still call me Zoe. I'm going to look after you like a mommy would, but you don't have to call me that." I reached out my free hand and stroked the side of her face.

"But I want to call you Mommy. Is that okay?" Her little eyes looked up at me with hope and my heart was completely melted. I pulled her into my arms and hugged her tightly.

"I would love it if you called me Mommy if that's what you truly want. I promise I will always love you Abby. From this day forward, you're my little girl." We hugged for a few seconds until a loud knock interrupted us.

"They're all waiting for you!" Silas popped his head through the door. "Are you ladies ready?" He winked at Abby as we made our way over.

"Adam has four best men. I think you guys can wait for one flower girl!" I smiled at Silas as we headed out to find my dad to walk me down the aisle.

"I'm not sure Loukas can wait much longer to get the party started!" We both laughed and I knew my life with Adam and Abby would be filled with endless parties, trips, and general shenanigans all because of his friendship pact. I was good with that.

~

PREVIEW - THE BILLIONAIRE'S HOPE

WEALTH AND KINSHIP - BOOK 2

APRIL MURDOCK

Book Two in the Wealth and Kinship Series focuses on Adam's brother, Silas Nicolis. Check out the first chapter to see how the friends show up to support him as he opens his first luxury hotel on his own.

CHAPTER 1

"I can't stress enough how everything has to be perfect this week." I looked directly at my hotel manager, Gisele. "This is our official launch week. Nothing can go wrong." She nodded back as we stood in the entry lobby of my most recent venture, Hotel Parádeisos, which had only been open a few days. She stared back from her tanned narrow face.

"I understand Mr. Nicolis. I have everything under control... it will be perfect." Gisele was a recent graduate of my family's hotel management training program, and she had passed with flying colors. As she was also originally from the Caribbean Islands, I thought she would be a perfect fit for my new hotel. So far, she hadn't disappointed, and every-thing had been running smooth like clockwork. She lifted up a binder and started flicking through the white pages. "Your personal guests are arriving today?"

"Yes. My brother and his wife. My cousin and two other friends should all be arriving any moment. The shuttle was meant to be picking them up from the airport?" I could feel my own nerves rising as I thought about their imminent arrival. I knew my family would only be supportive of me, but I still wanted to make sure that the hotel was as luxurious and sophisticated as every other Nicolis hotel in the family empire.

"The shuttle left an hour ago. They should be here shortly." Gisele ruthlessly crossed off her list and then shut the binder closed. "I have it all in hand. Enjoy your evening with your guests. I will meet with you first thing in the morning to discuss preparations for the competition." I loved how Gisele talked, she was like a robot. Everything was black or white, no grey. Her mind was completely dedicated to her job and I never had to worry about upsetting her. She gave me the peace of mind you can only get when you have capable and trustworthy staff.

"Sounds good. I'll see you tomorrow." I nodded as she headed off out of sight.

"There he is!" Suddenly I felt my hair being ruffled as my older brother, Adam, appeared beside me. "Hey, little brother."

"Hey, easy with the hair. I'm trying to run a professional establishment here!" I stepped back and laughed as I watched, Zoe, Loukas, Tanner and Zachary all walk into the hotel lobby. "You all made it!" I stretched out my hands and gave Adam an obligatory hug and then kissed his wife, Zoe, on the cheek.

"You didn't bring Abby?" I looked around them for any sign of my niece, but they seemed to be without her.

"Not this time. We decided we needed an adult vacation. One without waterparks and endless pepperoni and mushroom pizza – just the adults." Adam answered as he wrapped his arm around Zoe's shoulder.

"But you brought Loukas with you?" I winked at them as Loukas jumped forward and poked me in the ribs.

"Hey, I can be mature… sometimes." We all laughed knowing that Loukas was the life and soul of every party.

"Well, I appreciate you all coming out for the grand opening. What do you think of the place so far?" I couldn't resist but to ask them their first impressions straight away.

"Honestly, I think the entrance should just be one enormous cold shower, maybe a waterfall or something that would stop this unbearable heat. Is it always as hot as this?" Tanner stepped forward as he fanned himself with a flyer. Sweat was pouring down his forehead and his thin linen shirt was completely unbuttoned.

"It isn't that bad! You just need a day or two to get climatized." I smirked knowing that the temperature was only set to increase over the next few days, but I didn't tell Tanner that.

"You mean a mobile AC unit. Can you at least send us somewhere we can get something to drink?" Tanner was unimpressed.

"I can do better than that. How about I take you up to your rooms and show you around? Then you can get comfortable and chill out. I've got drinks and snacks waiting for you there. Sound good?"

"Lead the way!" Tanner motioned his hand and we all headed off towards the elevator.

"Your all up on the top floor. I'm just above you in the penthouse, but you guys have the whole floor to yourselves." We all squeezed into the one elevator, much to Tanner's annoyance. "Adam and Zoe, you have your own private suit and Loukas, Zach and Tanner, you all have the suit opposite." The doors pinged open onto the top floor lobby. "Here we are!" I showed the guys into their room first.

"Silas, this is amazing!" The door opened into a large open plan living area with large cream sectionals, a dining table and pool table. All of the walls on the exterior side of the building were glass which provided a full few of the beach and seashore below. Zach walked around the main room clearly impressed with the design while Tanner and Loukas headed straight over to the bar area. "This is really something Silas. Nicely decorated and what a view."

I smiled, glad to know that someone appreciated the thought and effort that had gone into the place. "You like that? It was one of the most important things to the design, ensuring that we got the best views possible from every spot." I looked out onto the deep blue sea, only seeing the horizon in the distance.

"Anyway, let me leave you guys to rest. Dinner will be out on the deck of the hotel restaurant. I've asked the chef to prepare everything on the menu so that you guys can sample everything. I want to hear your opinions on every detail, okay?" I looked over at Tanner and Loukas who were pawing through the snacks and mini bar the corner.

"Silas, we're here on vacation. It's bad enough that you dragged us all out here for our group getaway, we're not spending our entire vacation being secret shoppers so that you can pretend to be a hotel owner." Loukas threw a pretzel up in the air and caught it in his mouth.

"Hey, I'm not pretending at anything." I threw my arms out playfully as I knew the guys were annoyed about the 'work vacation' I had forced them to take. "This is my hotel, not part of my parents' chain. It's my first one hundred percent Silas Nicolis owned hotel and I want to hear your thoughts. It's not so bad... you have this exclusive suite, everything's paid for and you get to enjoy the beach. Now let me show Adam and Zoe their room. No more complaining!" I waved goodbye and headed back out the door with Adam and Zoe beside me.

"Just ignore Loukas. He's only annoyed because he wanted to go to Brazil this year." Adam patted me on the back as we walked over to the opposite door.

"Oh, I'm not worried. I've got bigger things to think about

at the moment." I opened their door and we headed into an almost identical suit that had a slightly different color theme. "I really could do with some feedback though about the hotel. I want you guys to try everything, do everything. Try the spa, the restaurants, order room service... I want to know any issues." As this was my first independent venture, I really wanted my brother's input. He'd grown up immersed in our parent's hotel empire and we'd both spent most of our lives living in luxury hotels and resorts. Adam eventually rejected the family business and made himself successful as a venture capitalist in New York. He'd only been married to his wife Zoe for a year and it was obvious that they were still very much in the honeymoon phase of their relationship.

"Oh, I have no issues with trying the spa facilities." Zoe smirked as she walked around the room looking at all the high-end furniture.

"I haven't even told you guys the best bit – we're hosting a wedding competition to launch the hotel." I leaned against the back of the sofa as Adam grabbed an orange juice from the bar. Looking at his wife and then me, he held the bottle up. "Want one?"

We each nodded and he reached in to get two more and brought our drinks to us.

"Thanks, babe." Zoe looked up and smiled sweetly at my brother. Completely out of nowhere, a stab of jealousy washed over me. Giving myself a mental shake, I refocused.

"Thanks, bro."

"So what's a wedding competition?" Adam went to the long sectional and dropped down to it patting the seat beside him for Zoe.

"Oh, I know. It's when you get poor engaged couples to fight over winning a dream wedding. You know, they have to answer questions about each other, or the groom carries the bride through an obstacle course. Humiliating things and then they win a wedding at a luxury resort all paid for. You probably don't know about these things because you've always been rich, but us poor people like to be humiliated before we get things." Zoe winked at Adam.

"Is that what you're doing?" Adam raised an eyebrow and looked at me with a concerned expression.

"Well, this one will be a bit different from how Zoe explained it." I rubbed the back of my neck as I wondered how best to describe the competition. I hadn't thought about it as poor people battling it out for the amusement of rich people before, but I could see Zoe's point. "It will be great publicity for the hotel. I want this place to be a wedding destination or THE wedding destination. The competition is just a way to get the word out about our wedding facilities. You can have your wedding on the beach with the water lapping in the background and then have a five-star meal at our restaurant." I tried to skip over the whole competition part and just focus on the benefits for the hotel.

"But you are having couples come and compete with each other?" Zoe sipped her juice as she looked at me.

"Well, yeah. We have to have some couples come and be part of the competition."

"And what are you getting them to do?" Adam again looked at me seriously and I could feel myself feeling nervous under his gaze.

"Um, I'm not sure exactly. My manager, Gisele, is organizing it but I think there's a karaoke round… maybe a questions round. Nothing humiliating." I had a vague memory of Gisele saying something about bouncy castles and mud wrestling, but I kept that piece of information to myself. I could see Zoe and Adam looking at each other with smug expressions and thought I might need to make some last minute adjustments to the slate of events.

"Look, you know how it is. We have to do these types of

things to get the hotel launched and at the end of the day, we are giving away an entire wedding. Some lucky couple will get their dream wedding completely paid for by myself." I knew I was trying to make myself sound more generous than I actually was. I knew that the competition was purely about getting publicity for the hotel, but I could help and justify myself to Adam and Zoe.

"Hey bro. It's your hotel, you know what's best here. I've never seen a wedding competition so it might be fun to watch." Adam could see that I was getting worked up and he tried to reassure me.

"I was actually hoping that you might help Zoe?" Zoe shot her eyes up at me, clearly surprised.

"Me?"

"I was hoping you might donate your services as a make-up artist to the winning bride?" I could see the surprise on Zoe's face, but I was hoping she would take it as a compliment.

"Sure, why not? I don't mind coming back here for another working vacation." She winked at me and then smiled at Adam.

"Well, enough about the hotel. I'll let you guys get settled in and I'll see you down on the deck for dinner?" I headed off towards the door as they shouted back their agreement.

∼

Want to keep reading *The Billionaire's Hope*?

Tap here to get your copy on Amazon.

https://amzn.to/2LYsdoR

∼

PREVIEW - THE BILLIONAIRE'S HIGH SCHOOL REUNION

SMALL TOWN BILLIONAIRES - BOOK 1

APRIL MURDOCK

Have you read the first book in the Small Town Billionaires Series?

Here's a preview in case you missed the series.

Want to skip the preview and go straight to Amazon to get it? Here's the link:

https://amzn.to/2GZcXYT

CHAPTER 1

"Is this the place?"

Blake Murphy glanced over at his best friend Travis, who was driving their rental car. Travis raised a single eyebrow at him, gesturing to the building in front of them, prompting Blake to answer his question. Outside, the bright Arizona sun was beating down, a noticeable contrast to the dread that was building in Blake's stomach.

"Yeah," Blake said, clearing his throat while looking at the building.

It was one story, built of plain tan bricks and sprawling over yellowing grass. Afton Bluff High School had never been very impressive, and this was something Blake had known even when he had attended school there, but he felt a rush of school pride even though he hated to admit it. Though he wasn't looking forward to being back here, he was reliving every ride back to the school after football games, every homecoming parade, and every team huddle.

They parked and Travis let out a low whistle as they got out of the car. Blake rolled his eyes at him, rethinking his

APRIL MURDOCK

decision to bring him along. It had been years since Blake had been home, always opting to have his parents travel out to his place in LA for holidays, rather than returning to Arizona. The town held nothing for him but regret, and every time the high school called him, asking if he could speak at graduation or open the football season, he always came up with a reason that he couldn't make it.

Not that it was hard to find them - he was a busy man, running his own company and co-hosting a talk show on ESPN with Travis, who was nothing short of a handful. Blake didn't know how Elise, his wife, could stand to deal with him. Every. Single. Day. The woman was a saint.

"She's a beauty," Travis said, laughing as they got closer to the building. Blake rolled his eyes but couldn't help cracking a smile at his friend's sarcasm. Travis turned to him, raising his arms and spinning in front of the door. "Does every high school look the same?"

"Probably. At least they all feel the same. Full of angst, memories, and hormones," Blake laughed, even as the nervous knot in his stomach was increasing in size. They stepped through the door and a wave of nostalgia washed over him so strongly he had to close his eyes and take a breath. He hadn't wanted to come back. It was only at the urging of Travis and the others at the show that he finally made the decision to get on the flight and spend a week in his hometown. A whole week. Ugh.

Blake could still remember the day he had gotten the call - his assistant had answered the phone while they were in the studio, saying someone was inviting him to come back to town for his ten-year high school reunion. Blake had immediately waved him off, telling him to inform the person on the phone that he had an event planned and wouldn't be able to make it.

166

Travis had punched him in the shoulder, scowling at him much the way he did when they had differing opinions about something happening in the league. Blake had seen that look during the last draft, and he knew it meant Travis was going to stop at nothing to bring Blake around to his way of thinking.

"Hey man, those are your peeps! You gotta go back to them, remember where you came from! You know, roots and all." Travis was emphatic, banging his fist on the table and meeting Blake's eyes solidly, his filled with conviction.

"I see my people plenty enough," Blake had replied, hoping Travis would just drop it and move on. "My parents are here all the time. You know that."

"Your parents aren't your only people." Travis had said back, launching them into a full discussion about Blake's hometown that eventually led him to confess the reason he didn't want to come back for the high school reunion, and the reason he hadn't gone back for the five-year reunion, either.

Trista Kennedy.

Blake hated thinking about her, and he hated thinking about how he had ruined his chance with the only girl he had really ever loved. She was probably married by now, living a nice happy life with a man who had been there for her. A man who listened to her and supported her dreams.

"So you've made some mistakes," Travis had said, hounding him just about every time they had come into the studio together. "It's never too late to fix them."

"No, Travis," Blake had said back, trying not to meet the other man's eyes. "Sometimes it *is* too late."

No matter how many times Blake told Travis that it was too late for him to go back and patch things up with Trista, he persisted, telling him that life was nothing without second chances. Though Blake had tried to hold out and ignore him, Travis had won in the end, and that's why they were walking through the lobby of the school building, the smell bringing back unpleasant memories for Blake.

"Hey, man!" Travis said, stopping and pointing to a plaque in the trophy case. Blake cringed as Travis pointed to a plaque and a trophy with Blake's name inscribed, a picture of the eighteen-year-old him standing with his arms crossed in his football jersey.

BLAKE 'BOMBER' MURPHY

"That's cool, man, I didn't know they called you that in high school, too," Travis said. Bomber had been Blake's nickname because of his ability to throw long passes. Trista had been the one to give him the name after a homecoming game junior year. He'd thrown two long passes that had both been caught for touchdowns. What a game that had been!

Blake cleared his throat, feeling more uneasy. It seemed as though everything in the high school reminded him of her. Even his own name!

"Yeah," he said, looking away from it, turning toward the hallway he knew they were going to have to walk down to get to the gym, which is where they were supposed to meet to help set up for the reunion. With every step he took, he was regretting his decision more and more. The thought of seeing Trista again, who no doubt was helping with the reunion, was driving his anxiety.

Why had he agreed to help set up? If he was going to come back for this thing, he should have just come for the get-together and let that be it. But no, he'd allowed himself to be coerced into doing this by his good friend and near enemy, Travis Bennett.

He and Travis walked into the gym and as soon as he saw her, Blake felt a wave of guilt and longing crash over him.

Trista turned around, a string of lights in her hand. He caught her forget-me-not blue eyes and took a sharp breath, trying to remember the last time he'd had the chance to look into them. Trista had frozen in her spot on the ladder, staring back at him.

Several other people were in the gym, all people who Blake recognized immediately. It was weird to see people so long after graduation - it was still them, but slightly different. A little older. A little more confident.

"Well," someone said in a haughty voice. "Look who *finally* decided to show up. We started setting up for the reunion *yesterday.*"

Blake looked over at Quentin Lee, who hadn't changed much since they had graduated high school. He still had stark black hair and black eyes, and a permanent expression like he knew he could do whatever it was that you were doing, but better. He also had a nasty habit of stressing too many words when he spoke, which made him sound overly serious. Blake bit his tongue to hold his temper in check, because all during high school he had wanted to bite back at him, but he never had.

"Hey, my bad. I couldn't get away till today," Travis said, in the way he did when he noticed tension and was doing his best to ease it. "What's important is that we're here now, and we're ready to party. Hey, man, you want to introduce me to your old classmates?" Travis looked over at Blake and nodded his head to get Blake to settle down.

Blake swallowed, nodded, and looked back at the other people in the gym, trying to gather some of the courage he had when he was getting in front of the camera, ready to share his opinion with the world. In the years since he had started his talk show, he had found that it had become easier to talk to people, but now, standing in front of his old class-mates, he was finding it hard to get out a word.

"This is Quentin Lee," Blake started, clearing his throat again and gesturing to the him. "And this is Leslie Fay."

Travis shook hands with Quentin and a blonde woman stepped out from her place at Trista's ladder. Her eyes were quick and suspicious, and though she shook Travis's hand, she looked as though she didn't particularly enjoy it.

"Travis Bennett. Blake and I work together." Though their history was far more than simple work pals, Travis chose to leave it at that. Blake realized he'd been rude for not introducing him and he'd had to do it himself. He was grateful for Travis' brevity given the oversight. He must be taking pity since normally he'd pay a higher price for forgetting the introduction.

Blake swallowed through the lump in his throat as Leslie's gaze swung to him, and she narrowed her eyes even further.

Leslie had gone to high school with them, but she and Trista hadn't been good friends back then. Blake wondered briefly if they were friends now. If so, that would mean Leslie had likely heard all about the details of their relationship and break up. Blake took in a deep breath and let it out slowly, then introduced a few of the other people standing around the gym. Travis shook hands with each one.

"And this is Trista Kennedy," Blake said, giving Trista a small smile and gesturing to her. She smiled politely at he and Travis, but there was something in her eyes that Blake couldn't quite read. He wished he could go back to the time when he always knew what she was thinking.

"Valedictorian," Quentin said, finishing Blake's introduction. "And organizer for the reunion."

Travis raised his eyebrows at Blake, looking between Quentin and Trista curiously. Trista smiled, but turned around and started focusing on hanging her lights again, rather than contributing to the conversation.

After the introductions, Blake turned his attention to the

state of the gym. Though Quentin had said that they had been at work since the day before, the gym looked shabby and sad. Blake met Travis's eyes and he had to stifle a laugh at the dusty, drooping decorations. Behind them, Trista had finished hanging their lights, but found that after Quentin plugged them in for her, only half of the string actually lit up.

Trista climbed down the ladder, frustration clear on her face.

"Alright," Travis said, clapping his hands and looking to her. "What can we do to help? What else needs to be done? I probably won't know what to do on my own, but I can follow instructions."

"Well," Trista said, sighing and putting a hand up to massage her temple, "there isn't really much more we can do... We're light on decorations to begin with, and what we do have doesn't even work. We've already hung most of the streamers and balloons. I suppose you guys could help set up tables and chairs."

Travis and Blake followed as Trista instructed them on where to put the tables, and Quentin and Leslie stopped what they were doing to help, both watching the two newcomers closely. Blake had never felt so studied in his life, and he'd played pro football and now had a career in television.

"Oh, sorry," he said, turning around with a chair and nearly running Trista over. She took a few steps back and met his eyes, and he felt as though someone had punched him in the gut.

"That's okay," she said, laughing and quickly averting her eyes from his. "I should watch where I'm going."

Blake felt guilt heavily in the pit of his stomach, but continued to work, running into Trista or accidentally meeting her eyes again and again as the tables and chairs slowly got put into place.

Travis gave Blake a look when they had finished setting up the tables, and Blake glanced over to see Trista shaking her head and looking distraught. He took this as a moment to really see her again - though she had always been curvy, those curves had softened since they were in high school. She was beautiful still, with long sable brown hair that fell in loose curls around her shoulders.

Blake remembered running his hands through those curls, and he remembered cupping her face in his hands and kissing her. Knowing he should refocus away from these memories, he wished desperately that he could kiss her again. Something in his chest ached for her as he watched her look around the gym in dismay.

"Trista, do we have another extension cord somewhere? And what happened to the banner that was supposed to go over the front door?" Leslie was holding yet another string of lights that looked worn out.

"There should be another cord, at least I thought there was..." Trista said, rubbing her forehead and looking around. She sighed and looked up at the ceiling. "There is no budget for this thing! It's like they expect us to pull off a reunion party with nothing."

Travis elbowed Blake in the side and Blake raised his eyebrows at him, not knowing what he meant. Travis rolled his eyes as Leslie asked for their help stringing up more lights, and the two men walked away from Trista to help. Travis gave Blake a meaningful look but Blake looked away, not wanting to acknowledge the fact that since they'd arrived this morning, Blake had been drawn to Trista.

"Okay, guys," Trista said, about an hour later. "Let's call it a night. I'm going to raid the shed out behind the football field tomorrow morning to see if I can find anything else we might be able to use to make this better." Trista met Blake's eyes briefly, then her eyes quickly cut away. "Good night, everybody."

~

Want to find out what happens next? Get your copy of *The Billionaire's High School Reunion* on Amazon

https://amzn.to/2GZcXYT

~

WANT A FREE BOOK?

If you enjoyed this sweet billionaire romance, I'd love to give you another one for free! Join my readers group and you'll receive a copy of *The Billionaire's First Love* as my gift to you.

~

Jack's back home after eight years away. Tracie isn't prepared to see him again. When she does, she realizes he still has her heart. They'd started out as best friends and even then she loved him. Can they pick up where they left off? Is life that simple? Is love ever that easy?

~

Tap here to get your copy of *The Billionaire's First Love*

https://dl.bookfunnel.com/ssfn7ng99x

ABOUT APRIL MURDOCK

ril Murdock loves romance, especially sweet stories that make you sigh out loud. She loves to write stories inspired by people in her life – past and present. Okay, so truthfully, she's never known a billionaire or anyone from royal blood-lines, but taking reality and pumping it up a bit is what makes it fun!

April has lived her whole life in the Southern US. Traveling is a great love, but coming home to Georgia where her heart is makes her happy. April is married to her high school sweetheart. Their children are married and they can't wait to have grandchildren to spoil.

~

Connect With April on Facebook

April's Website